NINETEEN SEVENTY-SIX

NINETEEN SEVENTY-SIX

A NOVEL

ROBERT DEWAR

Copyright © 2024 Robert Dewar

The moral right of the author has been asserted.

Apart from any fair dealing for the purposes of research or private study, or criticism or review, as permitted under the Copyright, Designs and Patents Act 1988, this publication may only be reproduced, stored or transmitted, in any form or by any means, with the prior permission in writing of the publishers, or in the case of reprographic reproduction in accordance with the terms of licences issued by the Copyright Licensing Agency. Enquiries concerning reproduction outside those terms should be sent to the publishers.

This is a work of fiction. Although many of the locations described in this story do indeed exist, the events that take place in them (other than those which are documented historical fact) are fictional. The characters named in this story are entirely imaginary (with the exception of the names of a number of anti-Apartheid activist Churchmen briefly mentioned in Chapter Thirteen). Any relationship any of these characters might bear to any real person, living or dead, is coincidental.

Troubador Publishing Ltd
Unit E2 Airfield Business Park,
Harrison Road, Market Harborough,
Leicestershire LE16 7UL
Tel: 0116 279 2299
Email: books@troubador.co.uk
Web: www.troubador.co.uk

ISBN 978 1 83628 013 2

British Library Cataloguing in Publication Data.
A catalogue record for this book is available from the British Library.

Printed and bound in Great Britain by CMP UK
Typeset in 11.5pt Adobe Garamond Pro by Troubador Publishing Ltd, Leicester, UK

For my Brother, Mark, who also loved Cape Town.

Chapter One

The building was now a residential hotel, and it shone white under the unseasonably bright early morning sun. It was an imposing Edwardian structure, with a jumbled roofline and tall chimneys, and it had once been a great private house. Built on the side of the mountain, it gazed out across a limitless ocean, beneath the vast inverted bowl of the southern hemisphere sky. On this near mid-winter's day, the sky was unusually free of cloud cover, and shimmered with shades of turquoise, cyan and cerulean.

In the hotel there lived, together with his wife and paying guests, a man in his early forties named Richard Channing. On this Wednesday morning the 16th June 1976, he had awoken with what had become, during the last few years, his usual sense of pronounced loss and nagging dissatisfaction. He groaned, sat up in bed, and glanced at his wife, still asleep by his side. Helen Channing, her long golden hair in disarray, her face bare of the least hint of the makeup she was apt to overdo as she prepared herself for the day, her eyes closed in sleep, was still a rather beautiful woman – if one ignored the sulky, dissatisfied set of her mouth.

When Richard married Helen in February 1958, he had just turned twenty-three, and she was only eighteen – and (he had thought at the time) she was a real smasher.

Helen had been born into the aristocratic and moneyed old Cape Dutch family of Du Bois, a family so refined that despite its having spoken Dutch for more than two centuries, Helen had herself been educated at the élite English medium Herschel Girls School, with its ties to the Anglican Church, and she and her parents had spoken English, rather than Afrikaans, at home. But Richard no longer loved the woman whom, as a girl, he had considered such a fine catch, and whom he had then loved passionately. The woman she was now (spoiled, superficial, obsessed with the trivia of fashion and appearance), irritated him – as did her small, black, yappy Skippertjie dog. The dog, Skattie, had during the night once again abandoned its cosy dog bed on the floor, jumping up onto the bed, and snuggling up against its mistress. Richard gave the sleeping dog a dirty look. He had never liked small, yappy, fluffy dogs. Helen knew that.

Although Richard was loath to recognise any redeeming qualities left in this woman he no longer loved, he might have counted the choice of the dog's name, "Skattie," as indicative of the saving grace of a subtle sense of humour on Helen's part, for "Skattie" ("Little Treasure") was a term of endearment in Afrikaans, the language that Helen's family had resolutely turned their backs on.

Perhaps, had Richard felt that Helen still loved him, he might have loved her too, and been more generous in his estimation of his wife, but he knew that he irritated Helen as much as she did him, and that she felt as trapped in a loveless marriage as he did. Why then did they not divorce one another? Richard told himself he persisted in the marriage for the sake of his son, Jeremy, who was seventeen years old (although Richard felt that he hardly knew his son anymore). It is probable that Helen told herself the same thing: as neither partner now spoke to the other beyond necessary and generally trivial exchanges, their thoughts on the possibility of divorce were unknown to each other.

And anyway, in nineteen seventy-six, a divorce was not yet as easy to obtain in South Africa as it was to become within a few years.

There was a knock at the bedroom door, and a young woman's voice, the accent that of Cape Town's Cape Coloured community, called out from the far side of the door, '*Meneer, Merrem*, I have brought your tea.'

'Come in,' Richard responded.

The young Cape Coloured woman, wearing a black cotton twill dress reaching just below her knees, with a white apron, and the stylised vestige of a white cap on her head, entered the room, wedging the tray against her hip as she opened the door. The initial effect her costume made was pleasingly old world (to dress the servants in this manner was an affectation of Helen's; Richard had only moderate fashion sense), but if you looked closer, you might see that the young woman's apron was not quite clean, and the vestigial white cap had turned a faded yellow from having been through the laundry too many times. The young woman – almost a girl – approached the bed.

'Good morning, *Meneer*, good morning *Merrem*,' she said, and she placed the tea tray on a bedside table at Helen's side of the bed.

'Morning Bella,' Richard responded to her salutation, thinking, as he always did, what a pretty little thing Bella was.

Helen awoke. 'Oh,' she said, blinking, 'is it morning already?' She did not sound very happy at the prospect of the day's arrival. 'Thank you, Bella. You can open the curtains.' Then she addressed her dog. 'Skattie my darling. Did you sleep well, my treasure?'

The dog yapped twice at being addressed by its mistress, and Helen kissed its pert little face.

Bella had drawn back the heavy curtains, and light flooded the room. Richard groaned a second time, but this time it was more of a subdued grunt than an undisguised groan. His wife looked as if she was about to speak, but instead, she frowned, her brows creased with displeasure. Those frown lines, Richard thought to himself, will set solid if she does that too many times. Helen sat up against the pillows, and poured two cups of tea, into both of which she added sugar, but she added milk into just one of the cups. She passed the cup of black tea, with two Marie biscuits on the side of the saucer, to her husband, and commenced stirring her own tea.

Neither partner addressed a word to the other. Sitting up in bed, they drank their tea in silence. In the oak tree beyond the wide, mullioned window, Richard could hear the Cape turtle doves calling "Work harder – work harder." It was not so much a lack of hard work which was the problem, Richard thought (although, to be honest, Richard did not apply himself to any great labours on behalf of the establishment), but a lack of capital. He lighted his first cigarette of the day, which brought another frown from his wife. Richard smoked between twenty to twenty-five cigarettes a day. His wife smoked only occasionally, and then only after dinner. At such times, she favoured the hugely expensive, imported, rainbow coloured Sobranie Cocktails.

The big house, which Richard had inherited in 1961 (along with a sizeable spread of land, although most of it was mountainside) from his paternal great-aunt, a relict of Lord Pitlochry, one time Governor of the Union of South Africa, was now maintained as an hotel. Richard had once had dreams (which still occasionally revisited him) of creating a select and luxurious retreat for the very rich, but so far he had failed to move on from the stage of two star residential hotel. He earned more from the bar take on Friday and Saturday nights (particularly during the winter, when he booked live bands and country and folk singers to perform in the great hall – a venue popular among a younger set on the weekend), than he earned all year from his half dozen permanent guests, and from the occasional transient. But even so, his revenue was insufficient to move the hotel any closer to the image he held in his mind's eye, of a luxurious and elegant retreat for wealthy foreign visitors to the Cape. What he required, he knew, was a large capital investment, if ever he was to achieve his dream for the Pitlochry House Hotel. But locating such an injection of funds had proved impossible so far.

Richard's prevailing sentiment now was one of disappointment: disappointment in his failure to achieve his dreams for the big house; disappointment in his marriage; and disappointment in his son – or rather, in the estrangement he felt growing between his son and himself. He wished to express his love for the boy, but Jeremy would not allow him to get close enough to do so. He remembered with yearning how close he and his son had been when Jeremy was younger, and he longed to share with Jeremy the youth's hopes and dreams, but his son, it appeared, did not share this sentiment. Richard wondered, as he sometimes did now, whether it had been such a good idea to send Jeremy as a boarder to Bishops, the élite private school the far side of the mountains, rather than insist that he attend the state high school as a day boy in Fish Hoek, the nearby town. But Richard himself had been to a well known English private school as a boarder (the school was known in England, where he had grown up, as a "public school"); he belonged to a class that sent its sons in particular to private schools as boarders. (It had been enough of a concession to the egalitarianism more generally prevailing in South Africa that Jeremy had attended a state primary school in Fish Hoek as a day boy). Thus, when Jeremy was due to begin secondary school in 1972, there had been no doubt in either parent's mind that he should have a private school education. Which meant, necessarily, a school on the far side of the mountains, really too far away to continue as a day boy.

So Jeremy had grown apart from his parents, in particular, from his father: Jeremy now had a rich life of his own, centred on school friends and school activities, a life in which his family hardly featured. The boy did not even always come home during the school holidays: often, he would be away visiting with school friends, whose families might live far up the coast, or in the Winelands, some distance inland from Cape Town. Once, he spent his holidays in July with a friend whose family owned a vast sheep ranch in the Karoo, over three hundred miles inland.

But Jeremy's father missed his son, and he had begun to realise that he would never now be as close to him as he had been when the boy had lived at home and shared so much with him.

When the Channings awoke, the African sun had not long ago risen at last above Silvermine, that great mountainous mass which loomed to the east. It had looked to be one of those warm, sunny days that occasionally intruded in the generally overcast, frequently damp, winter months of the Cape Peninsula, often accompanied later on by a "berg wind." But it is doubtful that Richard was conscious of the fine weather, or if he was, he was nonetheless thinking, "What have I to look forward to today?" He was certainly not looking forward to the appointment with his bank manager in Fish Hoek that morning. He was sure that the ordeal would be fruitless. He spoke at last to his wife. 'I have to visit the bank this morning. I'll pick up the mail while I'm at it.'

'I hope you aren't going to visit the Lord Collingwood,' Helen responded. The Lord Collingwood was the pub Richard favoured in Simon's Town, which lay some way further down the coast from Fish Hoek (which was by local decree a dry town).

'I might.'

'Then try not to drink too much this time,' Helen said.

To which there was no response which would not result in a beastly exchange of hurtful words, so Richard kept silent.

He sat up on the edge of the bed, and found his slippers. He went through to the adjoining bathroom, where he relieved himself at the lavatory, wondering whether he was developing prostate problems. "I used to be able to pee like a horse," he thought. "Is forty-one too young to have a prostate problem?" He must ask Doctor Fleming, the next time the doctor visited one of the old dears at Pitlochry House.

Richard and Helen took breakfast in private in a relatively small, but still tall ceilinged room, bathed in bright sunshine, known (logically enough) as the breakfast room. This was almost a conservatory, with large, wide windows on three sides, and potted ferns and other indoor plants in abundance, which was located at the eastern extremity of the ground floor, unfortunately, some distance from the kitchens (and from the big dining room where the hotel's residents were eating their breakfasts). Helen sat at one side of the table, her tiny dog asleep on the floor nearby, with Richard sitting opposite his wife. Richard's own dog, a well trained four year old Alsatian bitch named Katy, had joined the company. (Her name was a private joke: Richard had a younger sister named Katharine, of whom he was fond, but whose dog-like devotion to her older brother during their childhoods had been at times wearisome). Katy spent the night on her bed in the entrance hall, from where she could police the comings and goings of the household, and guard access to the floors upstairs. The dog knew not to come upstairs, but to wait until her master joined her downstairs in the morning.

Richard took a childlike pleasure in the three smoked kippers resting on his plate. How yellow they were! How delicious the flesh! In large measure, he had retained the simple culinary tastes inculcated in him at boarding school. Kippers (along with a choice of breakfast cereals, and porridge, and eggs boiled, poached, scrambled or fried, and during the winter, kedgeree) were served at every breakfast time, both here in the private breakfast room, and in the guests' dining room, largely because Richard enjoyed kippers so much. Having demolished the kippers, Richard proceeded to two fried eggs, turned over, with toast, fried tomatoes, three or four small beef sausages, several rashers of bacon, and a couple of fried kidneys – to all of which he added a large dollop of HP Sauce. Richard was a tall man, well over six feet in height, and broadly built (indeed, it was his impressive size which had first attracted Helen's interest in him), and his waist size was now four inches larger than it had been when, aged twenty-one, he had first arrived at the big house in 1956 in his Series I Land Rover, having set out from England to drive the length of Africa.

After exiting Egypt for the Sudan, the entire journey had been made in British colonial territories. Crossing the Limpopo River, he had left Rhodesia behind and entered the Union of South Africa, then a self governing Dominion enjoying the same relationship with Britain as did Canada, Australia, and New Zealand. Such a journey would today, Richard knew, have been considerably more difficult and far more dangerous, but every year, adventurous youngsters from Britain and Europe would still arrive in South Africa, having made the overland journey.

Bella brought Richard and his wife another pot of coffee, and Richard spread butter and marmalade on two more slices of toast. Helen's appetite by contrast was but a fleeting shadow, a wisp of a phenomenon: for breakfast she ate a bowl of cereal (she favoured Kellog's All-Bran) and a slice of toast with a hint of butter passed across its surface. Helen was thirty-six years old, and her figure was still that of a girl, but to keep it so trim, she exercised constant self restraint in her diet. (Her self-discipline in general was considerable; she rarely permitted her passions full rein – as Richard had unhappily discovered on his wedding night).

Richard made an effort to engage his wife in conversation: 'What are your plans for the morning, Helen?' he asked her.

'I'm going riding with Sonia Van Der Poel,' she replied.

'Uh,' Richard grunted. The Van Der Poels were another old Cape Dutch family, who owned much of Noordhoek, and lived not far away, in Noordhoek Valley. Richard was not greatly fond of them. He considered Charles Van Der Poel (another big man) to be something of a brute.

This exchange exhausted their breakfast conversation, and having drunk his third cup of coffee and eaten his second slice of toast with marmalade, Richard stood and – without excusing himself – left the table. Helen looked up as her husband left the room, and her mouth made a tiny moue. Richard still remembered sometimes that he had once loved his wife, but Helen had by now quite forgotten that she had once been in love with Richard. Her passions, such as they were, were now exercised upon her son (who returned them, up to a point), upon Charles Van Der Poel (with whom Helen was conducting an extremely discreet and secretive affair), and upon her horses. (She had three of these, stabled not in the old stables behind the big house –

to have reached anywhere decent to ride, you would have had to descend, and ascend again on the return ride, half the height of the mountain – but in the Van Der Poels' stables in the valley). Sonia Van Der Poel and Helen were old cronies, having been to school together.

Where horse drawn carriages – barouches, landaux, and Cape carts – had once been housed, several motor cars (in addition to one remaining Cape cart) were now garaged. There was Richard's Series III long wheelbase Land Rover, and a Ford Granada saloon, and of course Helen's soft top MGB Roadster – which her father had given her, in order to cheer her up, on her thirtieth birthday. There was also a twin horse transporter, and a little Austin van.

The Cape cart (with its two large wheels and a folding hood, it bore a relationship to what the British might call a "pony trap") was used only rarely, requiring as it did a horse to be transported up the mountainside from the stables in Noordhoek (the big house was located almost a thousand feet above sea level), but once in a while Richard and Helen would go for a drive in it together: Helen was generally happy enough to drive the Cape cart, and Richard counted it as good publicity for the hotel for them to be seen out in it together. Richard had another reason also for the two of them to be seen together in the pretty equipage: if (as sometimes happened) he began to feel that their faltering marriage needed propping up in public, he would suggest that they go for a drive in the Cape cart together. Helen would usually agree, and Richard would say something like, 'It will be good for the hotel's image.'

It was well known in the district that the Cape cart belonged to the Pitlochry House Hotel; indeed, the hotel's

Cape cart was the only horse-drawn conveyance in the immediate vicinity. Visitors to the district, who saw the Cape cart bowling along, the horse going trit-trot-trit-trot, might ask friends, 'Who does that pony trap belong to?' The friends might reply, 'Oh, to the Pitlochry House Hotel, of course. We must go there for a drink sometime.'

But Richard (who, in light of the unseasonably warm, sunny day, was wearing a Panama hat, along with a rather rumpled linen jacket, his old school tie, a pair of fawn slacks that looked as if they could have done with a pressing, and rather well polished brown brogues) intended driving the Land Rover this morning.

As Richard made his way past the kitchens to the back door and the old stables, he saw one of the cats that lived in and about the kitchens and the range of domestic offices, and which were sometimes found in the vicinity of the stables courtyard, observing with keen interest half a dozen or more Southern Double-Collared sunbirds feeding in the bottlebrush that grew to one side of the stables. Such lovely little birds, flashing in the morning sunshine like costume jewellery, and Richard admired their scarlet and blue banded half collars, the colours intense and iridescent. When he had first arrived at Cape Town, Richard had often found time to hike in the Peninsula mountain chain, and he had developed an interest in the fauna and flora of the region. In his great-aunt's library he had found publications detailing the plant, bird and animal life of the Western Cape, and he had learned to recognise many species of each. He still retained his interest in the natural world, but somehow he rarely got away into the mountains anymore.

Richard felt an attachment to his Land Rover, which he had bought new only a few years earlier. (He would be paying it off, he feared, for many years. However, as he had had the hotel's name, and the Pitlochry coat of arms, painted on the front door panels either side, the vehicle could be termed a work expense, and the monthly repayments could be written off against tax). Richard's attachment to the vehicle owed much to his nostalgic memories of happier days long ago, for at only twenty-one years old (when he had made his trans-Africa journey in a Land Rover in 1956), Richard had been gifted with plentiful self confidence and optimism (qualities which seemed to be much diminished now), and everything he beheld had then been pleasing and exciting. Memories of those happier times were intimately bound up with ownership of his first Land Rover.

Katy had followed Richard through the house and out to the old stables. She knew she would be joining him in the Land Rover. Having been trained by Richard at a very early age not to chase the kitchen cats, she considered them to be beneath her attention now, and she ignored the cat that was admiring the birds in the bottlebrush.

'Right-O, old girl,' Richard addressed the eager animal. 'In you get.' The dog jumped into the Land Rover.

Richard drove round the side of the house to the front, and then began the descent of the mountainside, via the narrow drive that was lined part way with eucalyptus trees only just past their annual flowering, although (much to Richard's pleasure, for there were times when he still possessed an observant and appreciative eye for Nature's displays) a few trees here and there were still in crimson bloom. The drive angled fairly steeply across the contours as it descended, doubling once sharply upon itself, and then continuing its descent, until at last it reached the gentler, south facing slope where several smallholdings conducted desultory agricultural pursuits. This land belonged to Richard, but the rents he raised from it were negligible, especially when offset against the costs of keeping up the hotel (the maintenance of its fabric and grounds; its staff and catering expenses), and the enormous expenses – her horses, her clothes, her jewellery, her car, her frequent and unnecessary purchases of pretty gewgaws and ornaments for the hotel – which his wife incurred. In the valley, Richard turned left onto Noordhoek Main Road, and about twenty minutes later, he had reached the outskirts of Fish Hoek.

Chapter Two

Fish Hoek was a middle class seaside town, for the most part occupying a flat, sandy valley. Behind the town lay huge, towering white sand dunes (the town's little boys would sometimes toboggan down them on large pieces of cardboard), and beyond the dunes lay some miles of waste land: scrub, *fynbos* and *vleis* (shallow bodies of stagnant water); a rough terrain (intersected by only one road), largely barren of Human activity, reaching westward across the breadth of the Peninsula (which was here very low-lying and narrow, and in ages long gone had been submerged by the sea), and terminating at the shores of the Atlantic Ocean. In front of the town lay Fish Hoek Beach. To the south of the valley, the lower slopes of Fish Hoek Mountain and Elsie's Peak were built up with fine houses (far finer than the more modest dwellings in the flat, sandy, valley bottom), many of them split level. The slow pace of life in Fish Hoek made even Cape Town seem dynamic, but this was nonetheless the Channings' nearest town and commercial centre.

The broad sandy beach, which shelved gently to the water's edge, varied in colour according to the light: the sand was either an off-white, or a pale gold. The beach was almost a mile in length, and it attracted both local residents and up-country holiday makers. The water was several degrees warmer, here in False Bay, than the bathing on the far side of the Peninsula, but bathing conditions could be marred sometimes during the summer months by a strong south-easterly wind blowing across the Bay. Fish Hoek's beach was not a surfers' beach. The best surfing was on the far side of the Peninsula, at Long Beach (which could be seen from the big house, high on its mountainside), where the Atlantic breakers rolled in to the shore. Although False Bay teemed with voracious sharks, including the much feared Great White, shark attacks on bathers at Fish Hoek Beach were relatively rare, spaced usually every few years.

There were many small holiday hotels and private boarding houses in Fish Hoek, along with a primary school, a high school, and churches reflecting a variety of denominations. Excepting the parish church of Saint John the Evangelist, which was Roman Catholic, these churches all represented various Protestant confessions. There was a fire station, a police station, and a hospital; there was a variety of retail outlets, and several bank branches (to one of which Richard was headed).

You would search in vain for a bar or an off-licence in Fish Hoek, for a local statute ensured that alcohol could not be sold in the town. If you wished to drink a beer or some wine in one of Fish Hoek's restaurants, you had to bring your liquor with you.

Running close to the shore, between the town and the fine bathing beach, was the Cape Peninsula Railway line, which connected – via many halts – Cape Town with Simon's Town, and so Fish Hoek was not only a town to which retired people and holiday makers were attracted, but one of Cape Town's satellite commuter towns.

Already, by half past ten, it felt remarkably warm for the time of the year. A hot, dry northerly – a "berg wind" – was picking up; a phenomenon typically associated with winter time in the Western Cape. The sky – now a faded, hazy blue the colour of kitchen crockery – remained cloudless. Main Road was fairly busy with passing traffic, and there were a fair number of pedestrians to be seen on the pavements. Richard left the Land Rover's windows down a couple of inches either side, and Katy sat on the passenger side of the car, and gazed at the people passing by. Richard had flush-parked the Land Rover, and he fed the parking meter with sufficient coins to give him an hour's parking. As he walked towards the imposing Standard Bank building, he greeted a couple of people he knew by name. One of these, a woman about Helen's age, who was as overdressed and over made up as Helen was inclined to be when she went to Fish Hoek, stopped Richard and asked after his wife.

'She's fine,' Richard replied. 'She's going riding this morning.'

'You must come for dinner again soon,' the woman declared.

Richard, who did not particularly like this woman, nor her husband (Richard liked very few of Helen's friends), made a grimace which might have been construed as a smile. 'That would be nice.' He glanced at his wrist watch. 'I must go now, Anna, I'm late for an appointment.'

'So nice to see you, Richard,' the woman gushed.

'Yes, yes ...' and Richard hurried into the bank.

Richard was feeling angry and frustrated as he unlocked his Post Office box to check for mail half an hour later. Yes – the bank had increased his overdraft limit, but they had not increased it by nearly as much as Richard had been hoping. And although he had raised the question of a loan for the hotel once again, the bank manager had not been forthcoming.

'Mr. Channing,' the man had said, 'the hotel's financial situation has not changed, as far as I can ascertain; the figures remain much as they were the last time we discussed this topic. I am afraid the Bank cannot see its way to extending the hotel a loan at this time.'

Bastard, Richard had thought to himself.

There was not much mail – and what there was consisted almost entirely of advertising circulars and those loathsome brown envelopes with windows in them. But there was an airmail letter from England, postmarked Gloucester: Richard could not think offhand of anyone he knew in Gloucester. He turned the letter over. Oh! It was from his cousin, Fiona. Later, he thought ... He stuffed the letter in an inside pocket of his jacket. The brown envelopes he threw on the floor in front of the passenger seat of the Land Rover (he had disposed of the advertising circulars in a waste bin in the Post Office), having caressed Katy's head and ears – 'I wont be long, old girl' – then he locked the car's door again, and walked the short distance to Sue's Café, on the corner of Main and Central, where he bought the *Argus* (one of Cape Town's two dailies: he had left Pitlochry House before having seen the newspapers delivered to the hotel every morning), and ordered a coffee, and a toasted cheese and tomato sandwich. Feeling a little better after the caffeine shot and the toasted sandwich, Richard made his way back to the Land Rover. The parking meter was about to expire. He took this – the fact that he had got back to the car just before his time was up – as a good omen. Of what, he did not know, but an omen of some good fortune headed his way soon. The dog gave a whine of pleasure as her master got into the car. Richard kneaded his knuckles between her ears, then started the car, and turned left into Central, doubling back along First Avenue, and so onto Main Road again, headed towards Simon's Town.

Helen can go take a flying leap, he thought ... the Lord Collingwood beckoned.

'Here we go, Katy! You like the Collingwood, don't you? And so do I.'

"What is the word I'm looking for?" Richard wondered. "Scintillate – that's it!" The ultramarine waters of False Bay, Richard thought, quite literally scintillated under the sun. One a day like this it was hard to believe that it was mid-winter. Richard had grown up and been to school in land-locked counties of England, but proximity to the sea never failed to enliven him. In previous years he had often sailed a small cruising yacht on False Bay, but although he was still a member of the False Bay Yacht Club, and the owner of a small sailing yacht, he rarely went out in her anymore. He did not seem to have the time – although, during his comparatively rare moments of honest introspection, Richard suspected that he could make the time if sailing still mattered enough to him. Instead, his son, with two or three friends (one or two of whom might be girls), sometimes took the yacht out on weekends in the summer.

As Richard, with Katy's window wound right down (Katy enjoyed putting her head out the window when they were moving), drew level with the first of the harbour defence gun emplacements located between the road and the shore, not far before reaching Simon's Town, he saw that there was activity around one of the guns: South African Navy personnel were obviously preparing a firing practice. Richard slowed right down, hoping to be lucky, and as he did so, there came a tremendous explosion of sound – a smack of pressure against the ear drums – as one of the guns fired a blank practice round. Sulphurous yellow smoke wreathed the cannon's muzzle. The dog gave a small bark of surprise, and a grin spread across Richard's face, an acknowledgement of the boy in him who had never truly grown up. He was deeply satisfied by the sound and sight of the big gun being fired. He saw traffic drawing near in his rear view mirror, so he increased speed again.

Now he was passing Admiralty House on his left, a building Richard admired for its elegance and simplicity of form. It was a plastered and whitewashed, double story, early nineteenth century structure, set not far back from the road, behind a fairly low perimeter wall of dark stone. The house had tall, evenly spaced sash windows set in its façade, the wooden window frames and the closely spaced mullions painted green. Only two narrow chimneys broke the clean line of the eaves and the shallow slope of the grey slate roof on this side of the house. The perimeter wall was broken by two wide gateways, with sturdy, heavily varnished wooden double gates, set between whitewashed and plastered brick Cape Dutch curlicues either side of each gateway. Richard, during his early years in Cape Town, had attended two or three functions (one of these had been a garden party) at Admiralty House in the company of his great-aunt, and so he knew that the front of the house (the ground floor sheltered by a cool covered veranda) faced wide, deep gardens running all the way to the shoreline. But it had been some time since he and Helen had been invited to Admiralty House. Had they fallen out of favour with the South African Navy admiral who was currently in residence? Richard thought it possible: he knew (because Helen had often told him so) that at times he drank too much now, and that when he did so (she said), he was liable to share his opinions too loudly.

Simon's Town, which spilled down the mountainside to the harbour, basked under the unseasonably warm southern sun, which today imparted a Mediterranean sharpness and depth of tone to the colours of quarried and cut stone, and pink, cream and whitewashed plaster, of the many varied and densely packed buildings – very few of them more than two stories high. The town embraced the only well equipped harbour between Cape Town and Port Elizabeth (a long way further up the coast). The port was steeped in nautical and naval history, and full of naval memorabilia, and for people like Richard, who had an eye for history's visible legacy, it was a fascinating and beautiful port. When he had first arrived in the Cape he had explored many of Simon's Town's historical buildings and sites, and to this day he knew Simon's Town fairly well, although now, most of his visits both commenced and terminated at the bar of the Lord Collingwood Inn on Main Road, which was set not far back from the harbour.

Simon's Town had been a Royal Navy base since the British occupation of the Cape in 1806, until being taken over by the South African Navy in 1955. The subsequent agreement between the South African Navy and the Royal Navy – in effect, a mutual co-operation pact – had only ended a year ago. Although Royal Navy vessels would continue to visit Simon's Town periodically over the coming years, the naval base would no longer serve the Royal Navy during times of war.

Richard flush-parked the Land Rover almost directly in front of the handsome Lord Collingwood Inn, a two story structure with a covered veranda between two slightly projecting wings, which stood right up against the road. Richard left the windows an inch down, against the sun turning the interior of the vehicle into an oven, and he and Katy climbed the steps eagerly and made their way to the bar, a large, cool room whose windows looked out onto Main Road, and whose long polished bar counter, at which two men were sitting with their drinks, was manned by a bulky middle aged man in a long sleeved white shirt with a black bow tie. His thinning hair was swept back from his forehead.

'Morning Richard, morning Katy,' the barman greeted the pair.

'Morning Rick,' one of the two drinkers greeted Richard.

'Morning Jim – morning John. Can I have some water for Katy, Jim?'

Katy had approached the drinker who had greeted Richard, and he was patting her and saying, 'Who's a lovely girl, then?' Katy's tail was wagging: she and John knew each other of old.

'Of course.' Jim, the barman, filled a deep, flat bottomed metal bowl with water and handed it across the counter to Richard, who took it to a corner of the room and placed it on the floor. Katy left John and followed her master and began to drink thirstily from the bowl.

'Stay!' Richard commanded the dog, who, after her drink, lay down on the floor, staring at her master at the bar counter.

'So, how are things? Your usual?' the barman asked Richard.

'Yeah, my usual, please. I'm OK, Jim. And you?'

'Oh, I cant complain.' The big man grinned. 'And no one would listen if I did.'

Richard laughed. 'That's true enough.'

Jim slid a cold bottle of Castle lager and a tall glass across the counter. Richard placed a one Rand coin on the counter.

'Have something for yourself,' he said.

'Cheers, Richard.'

Richard poured the lager into the tilted glass, held it to the light – that wonderful golden glow! – and took a long, deep draught. The barman poured a small measure of whiskey into a shot glass. He raised it to Richard, and swallowed it down. Putting his glass down for a moment, Richard lighted a cigarette. There were few pleasures, he thought, more enjoyable than the first drink of the day. The promise of imminent release from anxiety and discontent was like a balm.

John, who had greeted Richard when he entered the bar, smiled and asked, 'How are things, chum?' His rather long grey hair was gathered in a pony tail behind his neck. He was clean shaven.

'I had a far from satisfactory interview with my bank manager earlier. So yeah, things are much the same, John – and what about you?'

'Actually, not too bad right now,' John replied. 'I sold a couple of paintings yesterday.'

'Super!' Richard responded. 'Was it a private sale, or a gallery?'

'A gallery in Cape Town,' the artist replied. 'They say they'll take more of my work.'

John, like Richard, was English-born and raised, but he – again like Richard – had been living in the Cape for several decades. His paintings – mostly of Simon's Town's and Cape Town's various picturesque old buildings, although he did the occasional landscape too – were almost photographic in their detail and accuracy. Richard, with his eye for architecture, appreciated their verisimilitude, and he had bought several over the years, which he now had hanging on the walls in his office and in the entrance hall at the hotel.

By the time Richard left the Lord Collingwood at about half past one, he had drunk three bottles of Castle lager, perhaps one bottle of beer less than his artist friend – but in addition, he had had two chasers, both of them Irish whiskeys. The two men, who had known one another for a long time, began to laugh more frequently as their drinks soaked in. A number of other men had since entered the bar. (Although women were beginning to be seen occasionally in the bar, they were more generally welcome in the adjacent lounge bar). Richard knew many of these newcomers, who greeted both him and John. Richard was by temperament a gregarious drinker, and he enjoyed these visits to the Lord Collingwood more than Helen would ever understand.

Meals were served in the lounge bar between half past twelve and two o' clock, where there was a waitress on duty whom Richard did not know. She had been seen standing behind the bar with Jim when he had arrived, but had disappeared shortly thereafter. At about a quarter to one, Richard was suddenly overtaken by hunger, an imperative so urgent that he had to answer its demands immediately, so he had taken his drink next door to the lounge bar, with Katy following him. The waitress, who, Richard thought, was very pretty, was quite taken by this big, affable, good looking man, and to Richard's gratification, she was rather flirtatious in response. Richard ate a simple but well prepared meal at a table for two in the lounge bar, where three couples were already seated at their tables: grilled kingklip fillets with garlic seasoning, and green beans, spring potatoes, and a side helping of salad. John soon joined him, ordering grilled kabeljou with lemon. Richard was far from drunk – the meal had soaked up some of the alcohol – but nor was he quite sober. He recognised that he was feeling rather cheerful. What he enjoyed above all about alcohol was that the right amount of liquor obliterated the future tense: for a while Richard could live entirely in the present, free of anxieties for the future, and this was, for him, alcohol's greatest blessing.

Richard drove home carefully, his determination not to attract the attention of a police traffic patrol almost comically intense: as a consequence, he drove well below the speed limit, and soon gathered a string of irritated drivers on his tail. He was accustomed to driving home after a drinking session at the Lord Collingwood, and the traffic, excepting only when he reached Fish Hoek, was not challenging. But he had soon left the town behind, headed west along the relatively traffic-free Kommetjie Road. Before long he was turning right into Noordhoek Main Road. He reached Pitlochry House at about half past two.

"I'll put the car away later," he thought, feeling the pressure on his bladder of the three beers he had drunk, and he pulled up in front of the house.

Richard and the dog climbed the steps to the veranda, which stretched almost the full length of the house. On this unusually warm afternoon, several of the long term residents were sitting on the veranda. Miss Chelmsford-Spruce, who was sitting in a cushioned cane chair, a book in her hands, was nearest the veranda steps. She looked up as Richard and Katy appeared.

'Good afternoon, Mr. Channing,' she called out.

Richard halted momentarily and nodded at the old lady. 'Good afternoon, Miss Chelmsford-Spruce. How are you?'

His words were only very slightly slurred. The old lady smiled.

'Very well, thank you, Mr. Channing, although my neuralgia has been playing me up a bit.'

'That's too bad,' Richard responded, and disappeared through the wide front door. He stopped at the wooden counter to one side of the entrance hall, behind which a late middle aged woman, wearing a black dress and a white blouse, had stood up from her chair. Her greying hair was gathered in a bun. Behind her, keys to the guest bedrooms hung. There were few empty spaces.

'Ah, Mrs. Stoddart. Anything I should know?'

The woman looked at Richard, her expression fond. She was the afternoon duty manager at the hotel. A widow, Mrs. Stoddart lived in Fish Hoek. She started work at two o' clock, and would knock off at seven o' clock. Other than during the months of December and January (which was the time of year when casual short term guests were most likely to show), when a university student manned the counter, there was no morning duty manager: should somebody have to make a decision concerning domestic staff matters, or man the front desk in the mornings (for example, in the rare event of short term guests wishing to check in), the plan had originally been that either Helen or Richard would be present. In fact, there was often no one on duty at all in the morning, and in the unlikely event of someone being needed, the task would often fall to André (the husband of Elsbet the Cook), who fulfilled a multitude of functions at Pitlochry House.

'Mr. and Mrs. Du Plessis checked in, Richard,' smiled Mrs. Stoddart. 'They're a very young couple, honeymooners it seems, so I took it upon myself to upgrade them, and give them the green bedroom.'

Richard frowned. The green bedroom was a large first floor room with a view of the Atlantic Ocean, looking across Noordhoek and Long Beach. It was one of the few bedrooms with an *en suite* bathroom and lavatory. Richard seemed to recall that Mr. and Mrs. Du Plessis had booked one of the mountain facing bedrooms at the rear of the house, a far cheaper room than the green bedroom. But what did it matter? It wasn't as if they were inundated with people queueing to stay at Pitlochry House Hotel.

'Right-O then,' Richard responded.

Richard made his way past the stairs, to a doorway opening onto a cloakroom, and there he relieved himself gratefully. Entering the hallway again, he disappeared down a wide corridor leading off the entrance hall. He easily avoided any likelihood of seeing his wife: had she been at home, she would have been napping upstairs at this time of day, so Richard and his dog made their way directly to his office on the ground floor. This was located in what had been the study in his great-aunt's day; a room panelled from floor to ceiling in oak, and besides an impressive Edwardian desk of mahogany, there were several upright chairs, two comfortable leather upholstered armchairs, and a large Persian rug on the floor, whose predominant tones were russet, yellow ochre and dark green. One wall was fitted with bookshelves reaching almost from floor to ceiling, in which there were scores upon scores of books: there were leather bound editions of the Roman classics in the original Latin, including Cicero's *Orations*, Julius Caesar's *Gallic Wars*, Livy's *History of Rome*, Virgil's *Aeneid*, and Horace's *Odes*. (None of which Richard had so much as glanced at since having had to construe passages from several of these works at school; he had not enjoyed Latin at school, and he had avoided it ever since). Also bound in leather were classic volumes of eighteenth and nineteenth century English literature, and volumes of British history. There were several editions, some of them dating from the nineteenth century, of the fauna and flora of the Western Cape and the Cape Peninsula. In addition, there were contemporary publications on architecture, and maritime and nautical lore.

Furthermore, there was a large collection of English language fiction from the twentieth century, works which included volumes by Henry James, Joseph Conrad, Rudyard Kipling (including Richard's favourite childhood collection of stories, *'Just So Stories'*), G.K. Chesterton (whose *'Napoleon of Notting Hill'* Richard still found moving), E.M. Forster, Somerset Maugham, F. Scott Fitzgerald, Ernest Hemingway, Evelyn Waugh, Graham Greene, and John Steinbeck.

By far the major part of this library (excepting only the contemporary volumes on architecture, and maritime and nautical lore, and the more recent English fiction publications) had belonged to Richard's great-aunt and great-uncle. They had in turn found many of these volumes already *in situ* when they bought the house in the 1920s.

Against one wall was a sofa bed, on which were scattered several cushions, and it had a woollen tartan rug loosely folded at one end of it. Richard often enjoyed long naps here. Katy had a bed in one corner of the room (although at night she favoured her bed in the entrance hall), and she curled up in it, for she knew that her master would now almost certainly be taking a nap himself.

Richard had forgotten all about the letter from England, which was still inside his jacket.

Chapter Three

It was four o' clock before Richard awoke from his nap. His head hurt and his mouth felt dry. Tea and coffee were probably being served, in view of the warm weather, on the veranda today. Katy came and pressed her muzzle into Richard's lap. He caressed the dog fondly. 'You're a good old girl, aren't you, Katy,' he told her. 'You always know when your Dad's feeling rotten.'

He left his office and retraced his steps, Katy at his heels, making his way to the cloak room, where, closing the door on Katy, he relieved himself, and splashed some water on his face. Cupping his hands, he drank from the tap, gulping the water down. The water had a clean, slightly metallic tang to it; it was mountain water, stored in a small dam above the house, a dam fed by a natural spring, which had thus far never yet failed, even during the longest, hottest of summers. Almost certainly, so Richard had surmised many years earlier, the existence of this spring had dictated the precise location of the big house on the mountainside. Potable water, on the Cape Peninsula, was a precious resource during the hot, dry summers. There was also an enormous underground cistern beneath the house, hacked out of the granite upon which the house was built, the same stratum of granite which formed the lower half of the mountain's geological elevation. There were steps carved out of the rock in a descending circle around the sides of the huge chamber to the bottom of the cistern. Water was led from the gutters on the roofs to this cistern during the wet winter months. Lord Charteris (the husband of one of Queen Victoria's grand-daughters), who had built this house in the early 1900s, had got the idea of an underground water cistern from his time as Governor in Malta: so many of the *palazzi* in Valletta had water cisterns beneath them, storing precious winter rain water for use during the long, dry summers.

Afternoon tea was one of the highlights of the day for the hotel's long term residents. Miss Chelmsford-Spruce, the Doyenne among the residents, greeted Richard in her loud, fluting tones. 'Mr. Channing, is it not a lovely afternoon?'

And so it was. It was one of those near-perfect Cape Peninsula winter days that occasionally intruded in a season otherwise given to cold fronts, overcast days, and rain. Some people found berg wind weather enervating, but the mountain which reared up behind the house protected it from that warm northerly wind.

Mr. Carstairs, another of the hotel's permanent residents, had an inexpensive room high up on the second floor. Tall and willowy, still possessed of an impressive head of black hair (which rumour had it, owed more to the bottle than to nature), he had been someone in Cape Town's theatre world many years ago. He was always dressed smartly. Today – as on most days – he was wearing a navy blue blazer with brass buttons, a crisply ironed white shirt, an Old Diocesan Union navy blue and green tie, and grey slacks, carefully pressed by the hotel's laundry maid, whom, despite his relative poverty, he took care to tip rather generously whenever she delivered his cleaned and ironed laundry to him. He raised his hand and gave Richard something like a wave, the fingers curled. 'Mr. Channing, how nice to see you – as always,' he declared in a carrying voice which harkened to his background on the stage.

Richard was, in Mr. Carstairs' unvoiced opinion, a fine figure of a man.

Richard acknowledged neither Miss Chelmsford-Spruce's nor Mr. Carstairs' greetings, other than with a nod and a grunt to each. He had a sore head. Bella brought him a cup of coffee, and after a few quiet words with her employer, she disappeared, returning a few minutes later. She handed Richard a small bottle of Aspirin. Richard swallowed two of the tablets with his coffee.

There were ham and mustard, egg and tomato, and fish paste sandwiches being served, as well as a large Victoria sponge cake. Despite the hotel's parlous economic straits, Richard did not believe in stinting on the food the establishment offered. After all, he thought, it could offer little else. (In this opinion, he was of course mistaken: the hotel offered peace, tranquillity, and a stunning view of the ocean; for elderly and retired guests especially, who had had enough of the hustle and bustle of the World, staying at the hotel was an attractive proposition).

Looking around him, Richard could not see the young couple who, so Mrs. Stoddart had told him, had checked in today. Helen too was absent from the gathering.

Speak of the Devil! Richard thought, for he had just heard Helen's MGB Roadster ascending the mountain driveway, and it sped into view even as he wondered idly where she had been all afternoon. The car continued around the side of the house, and before long, Helen appeared from within the house, joining the group on the veranda. A number of residents greeted her. She and Richard, however, other than exchanging a mutual but perfunctory greeting – for form's sake – accompanied by a kiss each in which no actual physical contact occurred, ignored each other

A young man with curly chestnut hair falling over the back of his collar, wearing bell bottomed slacks and an open necked shirt with a jacket, and a young woman with long, straight blonde hair, wearing a short, tight skirt and a blouse, followed Helen onto the veranda. This must be the Du Plessis couple, thought Richard. He saw Mrs. Stoddart rise from her chair and lead the couple to a small table near the veranda's balustrade. As they took in the advanced ages of the other guests present, the young man and his wife each turned to the other with an enquiring look. Richard feared that they were thinking, "Have we booked into an old age home?" Mrs. Stoddart, who had been chatting with the young couple, now spoke to Bella, who shortly thereafter brought a tray on which were two cups and saucers – of tea or coffee – along with a pair of cake plates, a jug of milk and a sugar basin. The young couple helped themselves when offered a plate of sandwiches by Mrs. Stoddart, but they declined the fruit cake. The young woman was rather attractive, thought Richard, her long golden hair falling past her shoulders. She reminded him a little of Helen at about that age – there was the same long, blonde hair for a start – except that this young woman's face bore no hint of spoiled self indulgence, and she had a sweet mouth. Oh, Richard thought, to be young again, and in love! He got up and approached the couple.

'Good afternoon,' he said. 'I'm Richard Channing, the hotel's proprietor. Welcome to Pitlochry House Hotel. I hope you will have a comfortable stay here.'

The young man stood and shook Richard's hand. 'Karl and Sarah Du Plessis,' he said. 'You have a lovely place.'

'What an incredible view,' Sarah Du Plessis remarked, smiling at Richard.

The view was of Noordhoek far below, a patchwork arrangement of farmland, riding stables, trees (now bare of foliage) and scattered dwellings, and to the right was Long Beach, reaching as far as the small village of Kommetjie in the south, and beyond all was the Atlantic Ocean, bounded by a far horizon marked by the very slight curvature where the deep blue sea met a heavy, dark bank of cloud the colour of gunmetal; it was indeed a splendid prospect. Richard gazed at this outlook, one with which he had been familiar for more than twenty years, but of which he was rarely conscious anymore. There is a cold front on the way, he thought.

'Yes, it is,' he agreed. Out of the corner of his eye he saw his wife glowering at him as he spoke to this pretty young woman. Was she jealous? Surely not. Richard did not think Helen cared enough to feel jealousy anymore.

What irritated Helen was not that her husband might find the young woman attractive, but that the young woman

– her complexion so flawless, so natural, almost unadorned by makeup – might find her husband attractive. As, clearly, she did, for she was laughing and smiling with Richard as she talked with him. Helen was closer to forty now than thirty, and sometimes she could hardly bear it. She approached her husband, and taking him by the arm, she smiled artificially, saying, 'Darling! I found such a bargain at Stuttafords this afternoon! Wait until you see the magnificent coffee service I bought.' She knew that this would annoy Richard.

Momentarily surprised at his wife's sudden interest in him, Richard glanced at her (so she's been spending money again, the woman), before freeing himself from her grasp. 'Well,' he said, turning back to the young Mrs. Du Plessis, 'we will do our best to make sure that you and your husband have a super stay here. You will find we're livelier on a Friday and Saturday evening, with live music in the great hall, and people visiting from round about.'

The young couple perked up a bit at this information. Mrs. Du Plessis smiled at Richard again. She thought that the hotel's proprietor – so tall and broad shouldered, with just a touch of silver at his temples – was rather distinguished. 'I'm sure we'll enjoy our stay,' she responded, and her husband, rather left out of the exchange, sat down and took his wife's hand across the small table.

With a change in the weather in the offing, it had in fact already begun to grow cooler, and tea on the veranda began to break up as people moved indoors. A fire had been lighted in the great hall, and the air was redolent of the aromatic scent of burning pine logs. At about a quarter to six that evening, Richard took his double whiskey onto the veranda.

Talking to the young couple earlier, his interest in the view from the veranda had been reignited, and he remembered that it had been a long time since he had watched the sunset. But at this time of year, the sun set some way to the north of west, behind the mountain against which the house was built. Even so, a narrow band of cerise rimmed the horizon, darkening by degrees towards the south, until it could not be distinguished from the bank of heavy cloud above it – a bank of cloud that was already closer than it had been at tea time. The weather would certainly have changed by tomorrow morning, Richard thought. It had grown positively cold, and Richard turned and went back indoors, where Miss Grogan (pronounced "Groan," much to the delight of several generations of schoolgirls she had taught music to), one of the elderly permanent residents, was playing something rather nice, Richard thought, on the grand piano at one end of the big room. Helen was seated in a high wing-backed armchair upholstered in plum coloured brocade, sipping at a glass of white wine. Mrs. Hapgood, another of the elderly long term residents, sat nearby, a small glass of glowing amber sherry on the little table alongside her. Mr. Carstairs, with a whiskey in one hand, was chatting animatedly to the young couple who had arrived that day, his interest focused more on the young man than on the young woman.

Richard made a mental note to talk to Helen – yet again – about making economies. But now was not a good time: they were on public display, and the fiction of mutual accord (or at least, the absence of discord) had to be sustained. Richard approached the bar in one corner of the big room.

'Another large Irish, please, André,' he asked the Cape Coloured man serving behind the bar counter. The barman, who looked old enough to be retired, was the husband of Elsbet, the Cook, and lived with her in the servants' wing behind the house. He was wearing his evening outfit – a white jacket, black trousers, and a black bow tie. As it was a week day evening, he would be on duty until about nine o'clock. On Friday and Saturday nights, the bar stayed open as late as eleven o' clock sometimes, for then there would be casual visitors present, come to enjoy a meal, or perhaps just a drink, and during the winter they could listen to the live music Richard had booked. (Until recently, Richard himself had manned the bar on Sunday evenings, hardly an onerous task, but Mrs. Stoddart had known of a young Cape Town University student living in Fish Hoek, who now served behind the bar on Sunday evenings).

Richard, drink in hand, approached the grand piano, and smiled at Miss Grogan, of whom he was quite fond. She was one hundred percent *compos mentis*, and her wry sense of humour made him laugh. 'What is that you're playing, Miss Grogan?' he asked the old lady. 'It's rather lovely.'

'Thank you, Mr. Channing. It's one of Schubert's *Impromptus*.'

Richard smiled at Miss Grogan again, and went and sat in a chair near the fire, where, staring at the leaping flames, he soon lapsed into a brown study. How could he find the capital he needed to improve the hotel?

The hotel's long term residents had their meals, including dinner, in old fashioned shipboard style, at a single long table, with Richard seated at its head, and Helen at its foot.

Mr. and Mrs. Du Plessis, however, were given a small table of their own to one side of the dining room. They were the subject of many curious, and sometimes, doting, glances from the old ladies, for their status as newly-weds had got about. On Richard's left sat Miss Grogan. To Richard's right sat the Doyenne of guests, Miss Chelmsford-Spruce (who would have felt slighted had she not occupied what she regarded as the seat of honour). The remaining long term guests were seated either side at the table. They were all elderly, and, Mr. Carstairs excepted, all were female.

Tonight there was a new topic of conversation at the table (other than discussing the charming young newly-weds): on the early evening news on the single channel of television then available in South Africa, there had been a report of numerous deaths when the police had opened fire on a march by black school pupils and students in Soweto.

Richard had not been watching the evening's TV broadcast. He could hardly be bothered to watch the enormously forgettable light entertainment programmes which dominated the viewing on SABC TV. Almost all of them were TV series from America, due to British Equity's embargo on exporting British TV shows to South Africa. (In fact, he found some of the locally produced Afrikaans language programmes better made and more entertaining). By and large, however, Richard rarely bothered to watch television at all. But tonight, it seemed, he had missed a newsworthy event on TV. He would have to catch up when the morning newspapers were delivered tomorrow.

However, as best Richard could gather for now, from talking to Miss Chelmsford-Spruce at dinner time (her wits were in no sense diminished by age, and she could therefore be relied upon to render a fairly accurate account of this evening's news report), thousands of black school children had been marching to Orlando Stadium in Soweto, to protest the compulsory use of Afrikaans as a teaching medium at school, when the police had opened fire on them, killing a score – perhaps more – of the youngsters. (Later, claims were to be made that as many as two hundred school children had been killed).

Richard, like most so-called *"Uitlanders"* (foreign passport holders, who consequently lacked the vote in South Africa), was not politically conscious: politics in South Africa was almost entirely an Afrikaner closed shop. The ruling National Party had been in power since 1948, and seemed set to retain power for eternity. Outside of the name of South Africa's Prime Minister, B.J. (John) Vorster, Richard would have been hard pressed to have named a single Afrikaner governing party politician. He was aware that the United Party, then led by Sir De Villiers Graaff (who had inherited a baronetcy), a political grouping which had been in unbroken opposition since 1948, held somewhat more liberal views than the governing National Party. However, despite his lack of political consciousness, it seemed fairly obvious to him that these black martyrdoms would have troubling consequences for South Africa for some time to come. In fact, Richard had an unpleasant sense that things may never be the same in South Africa again.

Later that night, as they were preparing for bed, Richard (forgetting for a moment that he no longer bothered to talk about anything important with his wife) asked Helen, who had watched the news report on the television, what she thought about it.

'Uuhh …' she responded, her tone somewhat dismissive. 'I expect it will all blow over.' Richard felt frustrated at being unable to discuss the implications of the day's events. But then he often felt frustrated with Helen these days. He would get more sense out of his friend, John, the next time he saw him.

It never occurred to Richard to consider seeking the views of one of his Coloured employees the next day, for example, those of André (who, along with Mrs. Stoddart, was probably one of the hotel's most capable and intelligent employees).

Getting ready for bed, Richard had quite forgotten the letter from England he had received that day, which he had placed inside his jacket. But he remembered it as he was dressing the next morning, and he reached into his linen jacket, hanging up in the wardrobe. Today, in view of the change in the weather, he would be wearing a light Tweed jacket. He put the letter in the pocket of this jacket, and at breakfast he slit open the envelope with a butter knife, and began to read.

'What is that?' Helen asked him, voicing her curiosity.

'It's from my cousin Fiona, in England.' Fiona was actually the daughter of his mother's first cousin. Although they exchanged Christmas cards each year, Richard had hardly spared more than a passing thought for his second cousin in years, not having seen her since her visit to South Africa, some twelve years earlier – although as a teenage boy he had had a crush on her one summer.

'And does she have anything interesting to say?' Helen asked. With both Richard's parents now dead, a letter from England was rare enough these days to pique her interest.

Richard sipped at his coffee. 'It seems that her daughter, Antonia, is visiting South Africa, and Fiona asks whether she – the daughter – might stay with us for a while.'

'How old is this girl?'

'Let's see ... she was six when they came out for a visit in ... in ... uhh ... I think it was in 1964 (She was a sweet child, Richard remembered), so she's a young woman now.'

Helen was silent for a short while, while her husband continued to read the letter. Helen was pondering the implications of this development. On balance, she did not think it was a good idea to have a young woman staying with them. Her husband was so susceptible to young women. But there was little she could say, without the risk of sounding jealous. She could, however, legitimately ask when the girl was expected. She did so.

'At the end of the month,' Richard replied. 'She will be landing at Jan Smuts Airport on the 28th. She's staying with friends of Fiona in Joburg overnight, then taking the train down to Cape Town the next day – so she'll be arriving at Cape Town Station on the 30th.'

'Why is she visiting?' Helen asked.

'Fiona says she became entangled – that's the word she uses, "entangled" – with an unsuitable young man, and when that relationship went sour, Fiona decided a visit to South Africa would help Antonia get over it.'

Richard was rather pleased at the prospect of playing host to a distant relation whom he was sure would by now be a pretty young woman (for she had been a charming and very pretty six year old girl). He had been feeling rather low for quite a while. This was something to look forward to. He felt his spirits rise. He finished his breakfast in silence, the letter back in his jacket pocket, then stood, saying, 'Walkies Katy!' and the dog leapt eagerly to her feet.

The two left the house via the front door, and so down the veranda steps. There was a path hugging the side of the mountain which followed a contour for some distance. This path they took, Katy bounding ahead. Richard felt unusually cheerful. But when he saw the front pages of the day's newspapers at morning tea time (which Richard spent, as he generally did, with the hotel residents in the great hall – it would often be the first time he would greet his guests that day), he felt his mood darken. The papers had just been delivered (such a long haul for the newsagent's delivery boy on his scooter, up the side of the mountain), and Richard was scanning the distressing photographs and reports in the *Argus* and the *Cape Times* of the previous day's events in Johannesburg. (And these were just the photographs and reports the Government censors had permitted; Richard knew that the reality was likely to have been far worse). The government claimed that twenty blacks had died. Richard guessed that the real figure would be much higher. He feared that there would surely be long term repercussions of some sort. It was rare for Richard to be particularly conscious of political issues of the moment, except in the most general fashion, but yesterday's events had marked him with a sense of deep unease.

Later that morning, Richard remembered that he had decided to talk to Helen – yet again! – about the need for economising. He knew that it was really quite pointless talking to her about this, but some stubborn streak within him drove him to make the effort – a new coffee set, for Heaven's sake! Even as he went to look for his wife, his knew that he would regret any confrontation he chose to have with her. Nonetheless, he found his wife in the small ground floor parlour located at the back of the house – its decor savagely contemporary – that she used as a sitting room during the day. She was paging through a fashion magazine. Here, at the chrome and glass desk, she would attend to her fairly sparse correspondence; here she would entertain friends to coffee mornings, and games of bridge in the afternoon. This room (like their sitting room upstairs) had a telephone extension installed in it, primarily so that Helen could make gossipy telephone calls to her friends. She had very little to do with running or managing the hotel, although she would occasionally answer the telephone, if Mrs. Stoddart was not yet on duty, and if Richard had not already answered it from his office. Many telephone calls during the morning, however, simply went unanswered.

'You mentioned that you bought a coffee set in Stuttafords yesterday,' Richard said to Helen, by way of explanation for his presence in her sanctum. 'A "bargain," you said. I'm afraid to ask how much it cost. Do we need another coffee set? You do realise that the hotel is struggling financially, and that we're short of money?'

Helen glowered at her husband. A pair of short vertical furrows appeared above her nose. 'You are always going on about money,' she retorted. 'It's boring. It's not as if we're broke!'

'We're damn near broke,' Richard responded. 'And you're not helping much.'

Helen threw the magazine she had been glancing at on the floor. Her Skippertjie dog, responding to the atmosphere, yapped twice.

'That damn dog!' Richard exclaimed.

'You're horrible!' Helen retorted angrily, as she rose from her chair. 'I'm going out.'

'Yeah – go see Sonia Van Der Poel – go see your bloody horses!'

'Ai-eee – !' Helen shrieked, and stormed from the room, Skattie the dog trotting pertly after her.

Chapter Four

The overnight train from Pretoria and Johannesburg was late. It was midday before it pulled in at Cape Town Station. Richard had found a large piece of cardboard before leaving home, and using red crayon, he had written on it, "Antonia Bingham," and had stood waiting at the platform exit as people came past carrying suitcases and bags. He saw a very pretty, unaccompanied young woman approaching his post, followed by a porter with several suitcases and a bag or two on his trolley. She had honey blonde hair with a natural wave in it, cut quite short, and a heart shaped face, and as she grew nearer, he saw that she had large, lustrous blue eyes beneath dark, finely shaped eyebrows. She was wearing cream slacks and a dark green velvet jacket. He was sure that this was Antonia. He raised his sign board, smiling.

'Richard?' the young woman enquired of him.

'Yes,' Richard replied, beaming at her. 'Hullo Antonia. Welcome! You're all grown up!' What a lovely young woman she was, Richard thought, falling for her immediately.

The porter stopped and waited, and Antonia offered her face to Richard. He kissed her on the cheek, and said, 'The car isn't far.' Turning to the porter, he said, 'Will you follow us, please.'

'Meneer.'

'How was your journey?' Richard asked Antonia, as they made their way to the main exit.

'Not bad at all. Very comfortable, in fact. I'm impressed by South African Railways' service.'

'Yes – I enjoy train travel in South Africa,' Richard responded. 'Was the food good?'

'Dinner last night was excellent, five star. Breakfast this morning was spectacular, as we rolled slowly past great towering snow capped peaks.'

Richard smiled again. 'That would have been the Hex River Valley,' he told her.

Richard had parked the Land Rover on a solid white line in the station forecourt. When he, Antonia and the porter reached the car, he saw a traffic warden busy ticketing the vehicle. 'No!' he exclaimed. 'I dont believe it!'

The traffic warden, a middle aged white man, turned and looked at Richard, who, his voice raised, declared, 'This is too much! I was only away a few minutes!'

'I'm sorry Sir, but the no parking zone is clearly indicated, and you left your vehicle unattended.' The traffic warden began to walk away. He had placed the parking ticket beneath a windscreen wiper. It was enclosed in a little see-through plastic packet against the weather.

'What sort of person does a job like yours!' Richard yelled at the man's back. 'You should be ashamed of yourself!'

The traffic warden continued on his way, and without

turning around, he waved a hand over his shoulder. Richard growled.

The young woman looked on, blinking, at the scene. The Coloured porter, his face impassive, stood waiting with his trolley a few feet away. It was drizzling, and there was a cold wind blowing. Richard came to his senses, and said to his young cousin, 'I'm sorry. But it's too damn much.'

He unlocked and opened the passenger door, and taking Antonia's elbow, he helped her into the high vehicle. Opening the rear door, which swung on hinges on one side like a stable door, he and the porter unloaded the trolley (how much luggage Antonia had!) and then, rooting in his pocket, he tipped the porter twenty cents.

'Dankie Meneer,' the porter thanked him, and wheeled his trolley back into the station. Richard grabbed the parking ticket from behind the windscreen wiper and stuffed it into his jacket pocket. He was still too angry to feel much embarrassed by the scene he had made.

Antonia was rather quiet as they drove south along Rhodes Drive as it wound its way along the lower slopes of the mountain. (Perhaps she was tired from her long journey, Richard thought). They could see nothing of the view across the Cape Flats through the swathing rain (which had grown heavier), and the windscreen wipers were beating steadily. The young woman was hunched up against the far side of the cab, an empty seat between the two of them. Richard (who had quite calmed down by now) broke the silence. 'With luck the cold front will pass soon. It's not the best time of year to visit the Cape – our winters are always wet – but it's a beautiful part of the World.'

'Oh – the weather wont bother me,' Antonia responded. 'This is no worse than England – in fact, it's not nearly as cold as an English winter.'

'I hope you intend staying for a while, Antonia,' Richard continued. 'The winter will be over within another two months.'

'I don't know how long I will be staying,' Antonia answered him. 'I have no plans.'

Richard thought he detected a note of sadness in his young relation's voice. He turned his head and smiled at her for a moment. 'You are welcome to stay as long as you like. It's a huge old house. There's plenty of room. I run it as a hotel, you know.'

'Yes, Mummy told me,' Antonia responded. 'She says the house sits all alone up a mountain. I don't really remember it. I was too young when we visited.' Richard turned and glanced at her again, and found her smiling at him, a rather sweet smile. 'I look forward to seeing the house,' she continued. 'It sounds so romantic.'

Richard laughed. 'Romantic! Well, I suppose it is, in a way. Mostly, it just feels inconveniently isolated. But there's a tremendous view.'

As they climbed towards Constantia Nek, the pass through the mountainous spine of the Peninsula, the mist came down. Or rather, they entered the low cloud. But it had stopped raining. On the far side of the pass, as they descended towards Hout Bay, they left the mist behind. For a moment the terrain was lighted by sunshine, before the sky closed up again.

'Oh!' Antonia exclaimed, as she took in a glimpse of the ocean far ahead, beneath a lowering sky. A single shaft of sunlight broke through the cloud and glinted on the distant water. 'It is beautiful!'

The road levelled out, and bypassing Hout Bay harbour and the village, they swung to the south. 'We'll visit the harbour at Hout Bay some time,' Richard told Antonia. 'It's a commercial fishing harbour. Are you interested in boats? There's a super sea food restaurant we can visit.'

'That would be nice,' Antonia replied. As they left Hout Bay behind them, and began ascending Chapman's Peak Drive, the young woman exclaimed, 'My gosh! There's a leopard sitting on that rock!'

'That's Leopard Rock. The leopard is sculpted in bronze.'

'I thought for a moment it was real!' She laughed.

Chapman's Peak Drive was surely one of the World's most dramatic scenic routes. On their left, the road, cut from the living rock, hugged craggy cliff face and mountainside; to their right was a vertiginous drop to the rock fanged sea far below. Only a low stone wall, low enough to sit on, served as a barrier between the road and the hungry sea below. The narrow road wound and twisted, a delight for boy racers, and a driving experience which Richard still enjoyed, although the Land Rover was not the ideal vehicle with which to navigate the route. Occasionally, there was a short tunnel through the rock. Once in a while there was a lay-by, where cars could pull off the road and the view could be admired. Richard pulled in at one of these. Antonia could see far out to sea: it was the colour of pewter beneath the low, dark clouds, except for a single shaft of lemon yellow sunlight breaking through a rent in the sky, and turning a patch of the sea silver.

'What wonderful scenery,' the young English visitor declared. 'I suppose you must take it for granted, Richard?'

'That's why I enjoy showing visitors the Cape Peninsula,' Richard replied. 'I see it afresh through their eyes.'

After five and a half miles of this dramatic drive, the road began its descent into Noordhoek. Bare, leafless oak trees abounded. After a while, Richard turned sharply off the road to the left, and followed a single track metalled lane, which passed four or five scattered homesteads – smallholder tenants on Richard's land. Then the road became steeper, and they began their climb to Pitlochry House Hotel. Antonia began to catch glimpses, through the Eucalyptus trees which lined the drive, of the great house high above them. It gleamed white (the white all the brighter for the generally grey day), its many gables and chimneys creating (Antonia thought) a wonderful, jumbled roof line. As the car slowed and came to a halt on level, gravelled ground in front of the wide flight of steps which led up to the veranda, she said, 'What a fantastic house! What a wonderful place to live!'

Richard smiled, pleased that his young relation was impressed. Then it began to rain for the first time since they had crossed the pass through the mountains. Richard fondled Katy behind the ears – the dog had bounded down the veranda steps to greet her master – then he hurried round to the passenger door and hustled Antonia through the rain, up the steps to the covered veranda, and thence into the entrance hall, Katy gambolling beside them. 'I'll send someone out for your luggage,' he told Antonia. 'I asked them to keep something back for lunch if we were late.'

'She's a very fine dog,' the young woman remarked of Katy, who was now sniffing her trouser legs. 'What is her name?' She held out the back of her hand for the dog to sniff, which Katy did so, before submitting to Antonia's patting her on the top of the head.

'This is Katy,' Richard answered, pleased that Antonia and his dog seemed to like each other. 'She's a good girl – aren't you, Katy?' The dog rolled her eyes with pleasure. Antonia had risen even more in Richard's estimation: so many people were afraid of Alsatian dogs.

Mrs. Stoddart had recently come on duty, and was standing behind the reception counter to one side of the entrance hall. 'Good afternoon, Mrs. Stoddart,' Richard greeted her. 'This is Antonia Bingham, a cousin of mine from England. She will be staying with us for a while. Antonia, this is Mrs. Stoddart, our afternoon manager – and much more than that!' Richard flashed a grin at Mrs. Stoddart, who was very much aware that her employer valued her.

Smiling, Antonia offered a hand to the older woman, who shook it, returned the young woman's smile, and said, 'I have arranged a room for you in front, Miss Bingham, so that you can enjoy the view.' She looked at Richard. 'Would you like me to show Miss Bingham to her room?'

'No – we'll have something to eat first, thanks. Would you find Charlie and ask him to go fetch Miss Bingham's luggage from the Land Rover? He can take it up to her room.'

Charlie, a Cape Coloured man in his fifties, was the hotel's man-of-all-work.

'By all means, Mr. Channing.'

'Is my wife at home?'

'I'm not sure, Mr. Channing. Do you want me to find out?'

'No – don't bother, thanks.' Richard was not looking forward to Helen meeting Antonia. Antonia, he felt, was altogether too young and too pretty to bring out the best in his wife. 'Has some lunch been kept for us, Mrs. Stoddart?' Richard asked.

'Let me find out, Mr. Channing. Would you like me to have it served in the dining room?'

'Yes please.'

Richard led the young English woman into the dining room, an enormous room whose single fireplace was almost as big as the two in the great hall. At a small table, two places had been set. Feeling relieved (the table laid for two held a promise that Helen had indeed arranged for some lunch to be kept for the two of them), Richard pulled out a chair for Antonia, who sat down and looked around her with interest. The remains of a meal were being cleared from a long dining table in the centre of the room by two young Coloured servants. After sitting down, Richard lighted a cigarette.

'You don't mind my smoking?' he asked.

'No, I don't mind,' the young woman replied. 'Can you tell me something about the history of the house, Richard?'

'I inherited it from a paternal great-aunt,' Richard replied. 'She was childless, and I was her nearest living male relation. My great-aunt and her husband, Lord Pitlochry, bought the house in the late 1920s,' Richard continued. 'He had been Governor of the Union of South Africa. But the house had originally been built by one of Queen Victoria's grand-daughters and her husband, Lord Charteris, in the early 1900s.'

Antonia gazed at Richard, her lips parted, her features attentive. Oh, how pretty she is, thought Richard.

'How interesting!' Richard's young cousin exclaimed.

One of the servants whom Antonia had seen moments earlier, clearing the big dining table, now re-entered the room with a tray, on which were two bowls of beef broth and some bread rolls. These she placed in front of Richard and his young cousin.

'Thank you, Marta,' Richard addressed her. Marta was wearing a black cotton dress reaching just below her knees, a white blouse with the sleeves rolled up her forearms, black stockings with plain black shoes, a white apron with a frilled edging, and a small, stylised arrangement on her head, representing a servant's cap. Both of these latter were fairly new, and thus retained their gleaming white appearance. She withdrew towards the side of the big room, and stood there, her hands folded demurely in front of her.

"This is how people used to live in England," thought Antonia, who had dim memories as a small child of her grandparents' household with servants dressed not dissimilarly.

'Oh – would you like something to drink?' Richard asked her. 'Some coffee – water – a soft drink? There'll be some wine with the main course.'

Antonia smiled. How sweet she is when she smiles, thought Richard. 'You know, I wouldn't mind a coffee,' she answered. 'I had my last cup of coffee as we were travelling through the ... the ... what did you say it was? The Hex River Valley?'

Richard turned in his chair. 'Marta! Please bring us some coffee.'

'Ja, Meneer,' the maid answered, and left the room, to return after about five minutes – by which time Richard and his cousin had drunk their soup – with a tray on which was a well polished silver coffee pot (in which were a few small dents), accompanied by a small bone china jug of milk, a silver sugar basin also marked with a few very small dents, and two delicate coffee cups.

'Do you take milk?' Richard asked Antonia.

She nodded. 'Yes please,' and Richard poured coffee into her cup, followed by milk. He poured himself a cup also, but he drank his coffee black. He did however add one and a half teaspoons of sugar to the small cup. There was a silence for a while as they sipped at their coffees. Richard would like to have asked Antonia questions about herself and her life in England, but he was hesitant to do so, lest he touch upon a painful topic related to her so-called "entanglement."

The maid, Marta, had disappeared once again, but she returned shortly thereafter with the fish course. The fish was de-boned and flaky, and appeared to be prepared with a rich vegetable dressing. It was accompanied by sweet potatoes. After a few mouthfuls, Antonia remarked, 'This is absolutely delicious, Richard! What sort of fish is it?'

'It's snoek,' Richard replied. 'It's known as barracouta in Australia. The dressing is known as *"tamatiesmoor."* It's mostly chopped tomatoes, with onions, garlic and herbs. And of course there's butter in there as well.'

'How nice to live on the coast,' the young woman remarked. 'So much delicious seafood.'

'We are lucky,' Richard agreed. 'This snoek was almost certainly fresh this morning at Hout Bay – you remember? We passed Hout Bay on our way here. You couldn't find anything fresher. André – you'll meet him later – visits the fishmongers in Fish Hoek most mornings. Are you fond of seafood, then?'

'Oh yes,' Antonia replied. 'But I haven't come across fish prepared in quite this way before.'

'It's a Western Cape dish,' Richard told her. 'You wrap the de-boned fish in tinfoil, along with the dressing, and place it under the grill, or in the oven. It is always served with boiled sweet potatoes.'

Richard heard his wife's voice in the hall beyond the dining room. A moment later she entered the room.

'Good afternoon, Richard – and you must be Antonia.' Helen approached them with a smile. She was wearing a rather short, tight, dark blue finely woven woollen dress, which showed her long, shapely legs to advantage, and her face was, Antonia thought, a little over made up. Richard was tremendously relieved that his wife appeared to be willing to be civil. But then, she generally put on a good show in public. She had been carefully and expensively brought up, after all.

'How was your journey, my dear?' Helen continued. 'Such a pity about the weather.'

'Oh, I don't mind the weather,' Antonia responded. 'Richard was telling me that spring will be here soon.'

'I'm sure he was.' There was a very subtle edge to her tone, an edge which Richard recognised, but which he hoped passed Antonia by. Then Marta the maid cleared away the remains of the fish course, returning a few minutes later (during which interval Antonia and Helen exchanged a few anodyne words about the Cape Peninsula scenery) with a tray on which were two plates laden with reheated slices of roast chicken, baked potatoes, peas and carrots. These, along with a reheated jug of gravy (which, as a consequence, was very thick), she placed in front of Richard and his young cousin.

'I'm sorry the food had to be served warmed up,' Helen said, her smile just this side of a rictus, 'but we eat lunch at one.'

It was now some time after two o' clock.

'It's a delicious meal,' Antonia assured her hostess. 'I would hardly have guessed that it was reheated. I'm grateful to you for saving it for us. The train came in so late. It was so good of Cousin Richard to drive all that way to meet me.'

This was delivered in tones of honeyed sweetness. Ah! thought Richard, so the kitten has claws after all. He hoped that Helen was going to behave herself for the duration of Antonia's visit – however long that might turn out to be – but his hopes were not raised very high.

'I must leave you now,' Helen said. 'I have to get ready; I'm playing bridge with a friend in Constantia. I'll see you both at dinner.'

Neither woman had shaken hands. Nor had Helen actually extended a welcome to Antonia. But there were smiles – or what passed for smiles – on both their faces, as Helen left the room.

Chapter Five

Jeremy was in his final year at school: he was Head of House, and Captain of the First XI. But no one played cricket during winter in the Cape. He would be starting university in Cape Town in February next year. He had inherited his striking good looks from both his mother and his father; he had his father's height and broad shoulders, but was otherwise slimly built. He had his mother's golden hair, which, in accordance with school regulations, he kept cut in a short back and sides style. He had no great expectations of a school holiday spent at home, where he experienced Pitlochry House's isolation as a wholly negative phenomenon. On no bus route, far from the nearest railway station, Jeremy was cut off from his school friends, unless his parents gave him a lift at least as far as Fish Hoek Station, and collected him on the way back. Too young yet to take his learner's driver's test (in South Africa, you were not permitted to drive until you had reached the age of eighteen), Jeremy was unable to borrow one of the family cars. He often spent the Easter, spring, and Christmas vacations away with friends from school, but during the winter the weather was so chancy in the Western Cape, it was not worth spending the July vacation with friends away from home. His expectations of a dull three weeks at home were somewhat ameliorated, however, immediately he was introduced to his distant cousin, Antonia (who had arrived in the Cape only a few days earlier): what a stunner! And she was only a year older than he was.

'How long are you staying, Antonia?' he asked her.

'Richard says I should visit at least long enough to see the coming of spring,' she replied.

'Oh yes – the Cape is a different place once winter's over,' Jeremy assured her. Richard, who had made the introductions, stood and watched the pair: he was afraid that there might be a mutual attraction, and he did not wish to let Antonia out of his grasp. He could see that his son was smitten – like father like son! – but Antonia appeared to be cool about the introduction. That was good, Richard thought.

Antonia was thinking how good looking the boy was; she imagined that his father had looked very similar at that age – Richard's dark hair excluded. But, although she felt an attraction towards the youth, she had learned through bitter experience to be careful of good looking boys (especially, as she suspected of Jeremy, of boys overly conscious of their good looks), and she vowed to maintain a cool distance from Jeremy. So she smiled brightly at the boy, then turned away from him – almost rudely – and said to Richard, 'You said you were going to show me the family tree, Richard.'

'Let's have some tea first, Antonia,' Richard responded. 'I'm feeling quite peckish.' (Antonia, barely two and a half hours after finishing what she had by now realised were invariably huge lunches at Pitlochry House, did not think she could eat even a cucumber sandwich, were she offered one). It was tea time in the great hall. A fire was crackling and dancing in one of the two huge fireplaces, the scent of burning pine pungent and aromatic. Richard and his wife had just returned from fetching their son from school in the Ford Granada. Helen was busy chatting to one of the elderly permanent residents.

Jeremy looked momentarily downcast at being so casually dismissed by his beautiful cousin. He was not accustomed to girls ignoring him. He decided that he would mount a charm offensive. For now, however, he comforted himself with a large slice of the walnut cake that Elsbet, the Cook, had baked. Then he had a second slice, watching, out of the corner of his eye, Antonia with his father. What (he wondered bitterly to himself) can that gorgeous girl see in an old man like my father? He felt a sharp resentment towards his father. But then, he often felt resentment towards his father, whom (encouraged by the drip-drip of criticism of his father fed him by his mother) he judged to be a failure, compared to the fathers of his friends at school: his father was (he considered) an inadequate, who had not risen above merely owning a shabby two star residential hotel. The truth was, Jeremy was something of a mama's boy: he had been spoiled as a little boy by his mother, and he had become too early aware of his good looks, and he took his mother's side in the struggle between his parents – for struggle there was; he could see that much.

Since Antonia's arrival a few days earlier, she, Richard and Helen had been eating together at one of the separate tables in the dining room, and now that Jeremy was home, he joined them at dinner that evening. He quickly realised that Antonia was a good deal more sophisticated than he was: she had been to operas at Covent Garden, and to plays in Shaftesbury Avenue, and she had spent several consecutive summers with a family in France as a schoolgirl, learning to speak fluent French.

'*Mais c'est merveilleuse!*' exclaimed Jeremy, who was studying French at school, and wished to impress the young woman.

'*Oui, je l'ai beaucoup apprécié – mais ce n'est pas "merveilleuse," mais "merveilleux,"*' Antonia (rather cattily) corrected Jeremy.

Jeremy was quick to recover. '*Vraiment?*' he said, with a lopsided grin. '*Pardonnez moi, Antonia, je suis en faute.*'

'*Bien sûr,*' Antonia responded, smiling, rather taken, despite herself, by this confident youth.

Richard was trying to follow this brief exchange in French, but he had not spoken any French for years, and he was barely able to gather more than the general gist of the conversation. He did realise, however, that Antonia had put his somewhat forward son in his place. This rather pleased him. It was impossible to tell from Helen's expression what she was thinking.

But Jeremy was not downcast: "I'm in with a chance," he thought. Right now, however, Antonia was far more interested in his father: older men had never hurt her, and Richard was just as good looking as his son, but with a settled maturity which Antonia found even more attractive than Jeremy's fresh youthful good looks.

One Saturday morning in mid July, on one of those rare winter days of sunshine and warmth, with just a light breeze blowing – in fact, perfect sailing weather – Richard said to his son, 'How about we go sailing today, Jem?'

'I'm sorry, I cant, Dad. Mum and I are going riding at Roger's.'

Roger was one of Jeremy's school friends. He lived in Tokai, on the far side of the mountains. Like Helen, Roger's family kept horses. Jeremy rode well.

'OK … I just thought I'd ask …'

'Maybe next time, Dad.'

Richard knew that "next time" would never come. There had been no "next time" for some years now. He did not understand why his son resented him, but he knew that he did. This knowledge caused him much hurt. His son's distance caused him more hurt, in fact, than did that of his wife. Once in a while he would try to bridge the gulf between Jeremy and himself, but the result was always the same: Jeremy would spurn his father's attempts to draw him closer.

An hour later, Richard saw his wife and son make their way through the house, headed for the back door, which opened onto the stables yard and the old coach houses where the cars were garaged. Both his wife and son were dressed for riding; both looked elegant, trim, and attractive in their glossy riding boots, jodhpurs, riding hats and Tweed hacking jackets. Helen had used her own money to outfit her son for riding; she had not wished to offer her husband a chance of buying their son's gratitude by paying for his riding kit.

Richard felt a wave of loneliness and isolation break over him. All but one of the friendships he had made as a young man within the first few years of his arrival at the Cape had withered and died. (The one exception was his friendship with John, the artist who lived in Simon's Town). In the face of his family's rejection, he had almost no one now to turn to. He made his way to the veranda, hoping to find Antonia there, failing which, he thought he might visit the Lord Collingwood. On this unusually fine winter's day, several of the long term residents were seated in comfortable, cushioned cane chairs on the veranda, but the sun could not reach the veranda, which faced south, so they were well wrapped up. (When Richard had first arrived at the Cape, it had taken him a while to become accustomed to the fact that the sun followed a trajectory to the north, not to the south, during the course of the day).

Although Richard could not see Antonia on the veranda, it would be time for morning tea soon. He hoped that Antonia would appear for this ritual (an occasion much anticipated by almost all the residents), which, because of the fine weather, would take place on the veranda. Then one of the old ladies, Mrs. Hapgood, who had a tartan rug arranged across her legs, called out, 'Oh, Mr. Channing! Yoo-hoo – Mr. Channing!'

Richard sighed inwardly, and approached the old lady.

'Good morning, Mrs. Hapgood. What can I do for you?'

'Oh Mr. Channing, during the early hours this morning I heard a tap-tapping on the ceiling above my room, and a dreadful moaning sound. It was ghastly!'

Richard blinked. 'It was probably an owl, Mrs. Hapgood. Some of the glass is missing from the attic windows – that last storm we had, you know.'

Mrs. Hapgood had one of the least expensive bedrooms, way up on the second floor. When she locomoted, she hobbled, taking tiny, rickety little steps, a stick in each hand, and it took her almost fifteen minutes to climb the stairs to her bedroom. But she could not afford a room on the first floor, and Pitlochry House had no lift installed.

There had been a howling gale off the Atlantic one night a week or so earlier, and when Richard had walked around the house the next morning, looking up at the roof and chimneys for damage (it took some time to walk around the big house), he had noticed that two of the attic windows had panes of glass missing. When he had inspected the attics, he found the glass lying shattered on the attic floor. The panes of glass had been blown in by the strength of the gale. But he had not yet got around to telephoning the glaziers to order replacement glass panes, although Charlie, the hotel's man-of-all-work, had measured up the panes needed, and was capable himself of fitting new glass panes in the windows – had Richard only ordered them.

I must do so on Monday, Richard thought ... but I don't suppose it matters very much. Where is Antonia? Richard had last seen her at breakfast: Antonia joined the Channings for breakfast in the plant-filled, well lighted breakfast room. Marta had begun serving the residents their tea, coffee, sandwiches and slices of cake (a substantial looking fruit cake); age had not deprived the residents of their appetites. Bella was doing over the rooms upstairs, a task that took her the entire morning, so Richard helped himself to a coffee and sat down, gazing at the splendid view, a scene he was rarely truly conscious of anymore, for he had seen it so often before, at every time of the day, and in every mood and condition of weather possible. He felt himself sinking into a pit of despond. But then he heard Antonia's mellifluous, well bred English tones as she greeted him, 'Hullo Richard.'

Richard got to his feet, pulling out a chair for his young cousin, a smile of happiness and welcome on his lips. His spirits rose immediately. 'Antonia! I was wondering where you had got to.'

'I went for a walk after breakfast. I was away longer than I had planned. There was a path which I followed; it took me much higher up the mountainside, but eventually it grew rather steep, and I thought perhaps we could continue along that route together sometime.'

'I would like that,' Richard responded. 'It is possible to reach the top of the mountain via that path. But Antonia (his face now acquired a rather stern expression), please let someone know, the next time you head off up the mountain alone. The weather can be very changeable at this time of year.'

Antonia gave a rueful smile, the corners of her mouth turned down. Richard then grinned at her. 'But you're all present and correct! Sit down – let me get you some coffee. Would you like some sandwiches?'

'Thank you, Richard. And I wont head off up the mountain again without telling somebody first.' Antonia was still young enough to absorb Richard's small remonstration in good part, where an older woman, more wilful, more conscious of her dignity, might have sulked. Helen, for example, would have been angry at the criticism implicit in Richard's words, had they been addressed to her.

Antonia's face had an attractive, healthy glow; her complexion had been burnished by the winter sun this bright morning. 'That hike has given me an appetite,' she continued. 'But I must not spoil my lunch. I think I'll have just one sandwich and some coffee, thanks.'

Having fetched these, Richard rejoined Antonia at the table alongside the veranda's balustrade.

'I think I can count three ships heading south, and two headed north,' Antonia remarked after a few moments of contented silence while she ate her sandwich. The ships would shortly round, or had recently rounded, the Cape of Good Hope, which, although Richard knew it was not literally Africa's southernmost point, he still thought of as the divide between the Atlantic to the west, and the Indian Ocean to the east. In this opinion Richard was not alone: it was a common misapprehension, shared by almost everyone who lived on the Cape Peninsula. And the waters off the east coast of the Peninsula were in fact a few degrees warmer than the sea off the west coast.

'Why don't we visit Cape Town Harbour this afternoon, after lunch?' Richard suggested suddenly. 'It's such a beautiful day.'

'That's a super idea! I don't think I remember ever visiting a big harbour. Yes, let's do that.'

At half past two that afternoon, Richard brought the Ford Granada around to the front of the house. 'You're looking very pretty, Antonia,' he told her, as she descended the veranda steps. She had got changed just before lunch, discarding the jeans and checked brushed cotton shirt and navy blue cardigan in which she had gone for a walk on the mountainside, and she was now dressed in fawn slacks, low heeled walking shoes, a cream roll neck pullover and her green velvet jacket. She wore a yellow silk Hermès scarf knotted at her throat, and she had added a little makeup to her face.

'Thank you Richard. And you look like the archetypal English gentleman!'

Richard was wearing a Tweed jacket with a FBYC[*] tie, grey twill slacks, and a tweed flat cap. He knew from long experience out sailing that it always felt colder near the water. He laughed, somewhat embarrassed, and handed Antonia into the car. 'I don't feel very English anymore,' he said, in a self deprecating tone. 'I'm a Capetonian if anything.'

Instead of turning right into Noordhoek Main Road, and making for Chapman's Peak Drive, Richard turned left at the bottom of the drive, and followed Noordhoek Main Road as if headed for Fish Hoek, but after a short while he turned left again onto the Ou Kaapse Weg, the road which wound its way over the mountain through Silvermine Nature Reserve. As the road climbed, a vast, cloudless sky of electric blue above them, Antonia admired the wild scenery either side. The only trees growing once they had left the valley below were scattered invasive pines and firs, which had self sown and taken root in the rocky ground. These did not look in the least inappropriate in this mountainous

---

* FBYC: False Bay Yacht Club

landscape. For the most part, however, the terrain was given over to *fynbos,* that ecological system peculiar to the Western Cape, consisting of low, often aromatic, ground cover identified by tiny leaves and woody, twisted stems, and of delicate flowering plants such as watsonias, and of course there were proteas of every description, including the King Protea, South Africa's national flower. Only the hardy proteas, particularly the King Protea, were flowering at this time of year.

As they crested the highest point of the drive, they could see the dark evergreen forests of Tokai below them, and off to the right was Muizenberg with its beach on the shores of False Bay. Beyond them the Cape Flats reached out to the far mountain ranges that served as a barrier to the hinterland.

'What a stupendous view!' declared Antonia.

'Yes,' Richard responded. 'I love the Cape. It's "home" for me now.' The road described a hairpin bend, descending rapidly.

'How long have you lived out here?' Antonia asked.

'Since '56,' Richard replied. 'I've almost forgotten England.'

They sped north along the Simon Van Der Stel Freeway (which almost everyone, for some obscure reason, referred to as "The Blue Route"), with distant Constantiaberg looming against the horizon to their left, and on either side of the freeway, new white residential suburbs were being built, where not long before, vineyards had flourished. The Back Table system drew nearer and nearer, until in time they were winding their way along the side of the mountain, as they followed Rhodes Drive into Cape Town.

They passed the University of Cape Town on their left, laid out in a series of broad, descending terraces; surely no other university campus anywhere in the World could match its mountainside location, with its magnificent view across the Cape Flats to far distant mountain ranges. Richard had not long ago visited the university with Helen, curious to see where Jeremy (who had already enjoyed a tour of the university, organised by his school) would be a student next year.

That excursion had been one of the very few occasions that Richard and Helen had gone out together somewhere – united as they were in a common concern for their son. Once in a while they were invited to a garden party, or a dinner party, and very occasionally, they would go for a drive together in the Cape cart, but the occasions when Richard and his wife chose to spend time together away from home were few – as indeed were the occasions, mealtimes and nigthttimes excluded, when they chose to spend any time together at home.

Crossing the city centre via Strand Street (which had once marked the shoreline, a shoreline now in far distant retreat due to land reclamation over the years), Richard turned right into Buitengracht Street, heading for the docks. At the bottom of Buitengracht Street, Richard turned left into Dock Road, and almost immediately, he came up to the Customs barrier, but entering the Harbour precinct, he was merely waved through. Shortly thereafter, a small steam shunting engine held them up as it crossed the road, trailing a line of wagons: woof-woof-woof-woof-hsssshh-clang-bash! Antonia felt an almost childlike interest and excitement in the scene as she took it in, her lips parted. The steam shunter halted, the line of wagons blocking the road, then the wagons, having cleared a switching point, began to reverse, followed by the shunting engine again, itself now in reverse. Then their way was clear. Ahead, their metal frames towering above the warehouses and other buildings which impeded a direct view of the quayside, could be seen enormously high dockside cranes, one of which was in motion, its massive gantry swinging slowly round. Despite it being a Saturday afternoon, the docks were still fairly busy. A lorry, a tarpaulin covering its load, passed by them, and through her open window, Antonia could hear a distant shunting engine's chuff-chuff-chuff, and the percussive crash of its wagons and their couplings. Then she heard a ship's deep toned, booming steam whistle which momentarily overwhelmed all the other dockside noises. Richard parked the car in front of a warehouse at the quayside.

'Let's walk,' he said. On the quayside, Antonia slipped her arm through Richard's, the first time she had permitted such intimate physical contact with him. Richard felt a thrill at this expression of familiarity and trust on her part.

The quayside was littered with commercial *bric-à-brac*: there were drums of some flammable liquid (Antonia could see the stencilled and spray-painted stylised images of warning flames in red on their sides); huge wooden crates whose contents Antonia could only guess at; large wooden pallets stacked one upon another; mounds of nameless goods beneath tarpaulin covers; and set into the fissured, oily concrete paved surface were deep grooved, wide edged steel rails, the tracks along which the harbour-side cranes travelled. The air smelled of coal smoke from the steam shunting engines at work in the harbour, and beneath that was the briny tang of the sea, with overtones of bunker and lubricating oil, and of unknown, pungent scents from the nameless stacks of canvas covered cargo scattered seemingly haphazardly on the quayside.

The quayside itself was lined with cargo vessels, moored along their portsides against the quay: big ocean going ships, from the bows and sterns of which, massive hawsers reached to huge solid iron mooring bollards set into the quay. Great circular barriers against rats – as much to prevent diseased rats from gaining the land, as to prevent Cape Town rats from stowing away aboard ship – wooden discs of almost three feet in diameter, were set halfway up these heavy mooring hawsers. From one of these ships, a vessel with an unpronounceable Polish name painted at its bows, a trio of sailors – rough looking men who had refrained from shaving for some days – leant over the ship's railing from high above them, and called out merry (and quite likely, ribald) comments in – presumably – Polish, comments which reduced the sailors to coarse laughter as Richard and the very pretty young woman passed by below them. Richard drew Antonia closer to him.

Richard found the ships and the dockside activities fascinating. He had always been drawn to busy commercial and fishing harbours, to ships and boats. But Antonia by now was finding the scene somewhat overwhelming and just a little frightening: those towering harbour cranes moving slowly, seemingly inexorably, along their rails; the steam shunting engine pushing a row of wagons which passed behind them not more than twenty feet away, with a tremendous sound of clanging couplings, echoing back at them from the warehouses they were passing. She was relieved when Richard (their having walked almost the entire length of the Duncan Dock's quayside, then turned around and begun their walk back again) said, 'We'll visit the Royal Cape Yacht Club. I dont know about you, but I would enjoy a drink about now.'

Looking at her wristwatch, Antonia was surprised to find that it was soon after five o' clock. The sun was quite low in the sky, and the air – a cold wind had come up within the last ten minutes – had suddenly acquired a bite to it.

'That's a very good idea,' she responded.

They got into the car and drove the length of the Duncan Dock (a distance most of which they had already covered on foot). Occasionally they would have to make their way around lorries in their path, busy unloading or being loaded, but for the most part following a route clear of obstacles, an area between the inset rails used by the steam shunting engines and their wagons, and the row of warehouses set back from the quayside. They entered the premises of the Royal Cape Yacht Club via a side gate, parking in front of the clubhouse complex.

The RCYC was an aristocratic institution, affiliated membership of which Richard enjoyed, by virtue of his membership of the FBYC at Simon's Town. But in the bar (where Richard was not alone in wearing a jacket and tie), they were not asked to establish their *bona fides*, but were served without question by the white jacketed Cape Coloured barman. Perhaps the man had noted Richard's

FBYC tie. Richard ordered the large Irish whiskey he felt by now he needed (the sun, after all, was well over the yardarm!), and the Cinzano *Rosso* with lemonade that Antonia (feeling, at only eighteen years old, after all, quite sophisticated) had requested of him.

'Cheers!' Richard declared, raising his glass and gulping at it.

'Cheers,' Antonia responded, and sipped somewhat more demurely at her Cinzano *Rosso*. She heard the low murmur of voices around her in the large room, with now and then a sudden burst of laughter, and soft piped music in the background, and the room felt warm and safe, and she was content in Richard's company.

Chapter Six

During the drive back, Richard fortified with two large Irish whiskeys, Antonia – as a consequence of the two Cinzanos she had drunk – was inclined to indulge in light hearted quips, which Richard thought were quite charming. He felt that he had scored a hit with his lovely young cousin that afternoon. (And she was, Richard considered, distantly enough related for her to be, if not quite fair game, then at least a prospect for a harmless dalliance. Richard had never yet been unfaithful to Helen in the absolute sense, and it is doubtful that he imagined betraying his marriage vows – even if he were able – now). As they began their descent of the far side of Silvermine, the western sky – a vast canvas for Nature's brush – still showed the diminishing glow of the earlier sunset, with an array of high clouds washed with faded pink and orange. It was now after half past six, and the sun at this time of year set at six o' clock. They caught occasional glimpses of lights twinkling far below. Richard had the car's heater turned on: the air had grown very cold, for a bitter wind had picked up. Richard doubted the weather would be as pleasant tomorrow as it had been today.

At Pitlochry House, Richard drove round the side of the house to the old stables at the back, where he saw Helen's roadster parked, and after he had garaged the Ford Granada, he and Antonia entered the house via the back door. As they passed the kitchens, Antonia touched Richard's arm lightly.

'I had a super time. Thanks, Richard.'

Richard reached his hand across and trapped her hand on his forearm for a moment.

'I enjoyed myself too.'

Katy greeted her master joyfully in the entrance hall. Richard caressed the dog's head and ears. 'Have you been a good girl, then?' he asked. The dog's tail wagged fast. Richard and Antonia entered the great hall, and Richard approached the bar located in one corner of the big double story room.

'Good evening, André,' he greeted the barman.

'Good evening, Mr. Channing,' the barman replied.

Richard turned to Antonia. 'Would you like anything, to drink, Antonia?'

'Oh – no thanks. I'll wait 'till dinner, Richard.'

At that moment, Helen entered the room. She was elegantly dressed in a raw silk cocktail dress of pale yellow, which displayed her slim figure and long legs to advantage. She tended to dress up on Friday and Saturday evenings: there would be visitors arriving later that evening, to hear the live music act that Richard had booked for this weekend. The act tonight was a duo: a male guitarist and a female folk singer, and they had been well received the night before. They would be arriving during dinner, and would have time for a drink or two in the great hall, compliments of Pitlochry House Hotel, before beginning their act.

Helen looked healthy and vital after her energetic, lengthy ride in Tokai with her son that morning, her complexion (as was that of Antonia, for that matter) enhanced by the soft yellow lighting in the great hall. But her bare shoulders, thought Antonia, looked cold.

'Good evening,' Helen addressed the room's occupants in general. (Most of the hotel's guests were seated there, enjoying the fire, although the majority would retire to the residents' lounge and the television after dinner, rather than return to the great hall for the live music). 'Good evening, Antonia,' she said, ignoring her husband. 'Did you have a nice time?'

'Yes, thank you, Helen, I enjoyed myself. The harbour was fascinating, and I enjoyed the drive there and back too.'

Helen smiled mechanically at Antonia, then gave her husband a quick, analytical glance, a glance of such clinical precision that she was able to establish that he had already enjoyed several drinks while out. His features radiated good cheer. This irritated his wife. He was growing altogether too close, she thought, to this attractive English girl. While she herself felt little desire for Richard's attentions anymore, she did not wish him to enjoy the attentions of others, particularly when the others were female, and young and attractive.

The following morning, a Sunday, Jeremy (who was feeling somewhat hung-over, for the evening before he had managed to escape his mother's attentions long enough to down several beers while listening to the live music in the great hall), at his mother's suggestion, prevailed upon Antonia to come riding with them at the Van Der Poel stables in Noordhoek. Aged only seventeen, Jeremy was not yet old enough in South Africa to possess a driver's licence, and he had to rely largely on his doting mother, or slightly older friends, for transport. That would change the following year. Richard was already anticipating the expense of obtaining a small sports car for his son.

'You do ride, don't you, Antonia?' the boy asked her.

'Of course. But I haven't anything suitable to wear,' Antonia answered.

'Oh – jeans and ordinary shoes will do,' Jeremy responded.

'OK,' the young woman said. 'Let me go upstairs and change.'

When Antonia came back downstairs, she had discarded her dress in favour of a pair of blue jeans which hugged her figure as far as her knees, where they began to flare out. ("Flares," or "bell-bottoms," were then fashionable). She had swapped her shoes for a pair of sneakers, and beneath a short brown leather jacket, she wore a brushed cotton lumberjack shirt in a red and grey check, tucked into her jeans, for it was much cooler today. Her honey blonde hair was hidden by a silk scarf. She looked, thought Jeremy, the epitome of an athletic outdoors girl.

Jeremy was wearing a beautifully tailored brown Tweed jacket, with jeans and a pair of chukka boots. He carried a Tweed cap in one hand. He was, Antonia thought, looking rather handsome; fresh faced and youthful, his short golden hair shining.

"I must not fall for him," she thought. Painful memories of Toby, the beautiful young man who had hurt her so much in England, still intruded often in her thoughts. But as they walked down the veranda steps towards the waiting car, Richard could hear the two young people laughing. He felt a spurt of hot jealousy.

Helen was waiting for them in the Ford Granada (Helen's MGB Roadster could not carry three people), and she was dressed down for this Sunday morning visit to the stables: she too was wearing jeans, chukka boots, a Tweed hacking jacket, and a capacious woollen hat, in which her long blonde hair, the same pale gold as her son's, had been gathered.

Richard took Katy for a long walk, returning a long time after morning tea was over, and he sneaked inside via the back door, and retreated to his office, for he was not in the mood for talking to his guests. Katy curled up in her bed, and Richard sat down in the comfortable leather armchair, a novel on his lap, *The Eagle has Landed*, by Jack Higgins, published the previous year. In a drawer in the desk he kept a bottle of Bushmills, which he placed on the small table alongside him, together with a whiskey tumbler, and he sipped at the whiskey and smoked while he read. He was not entirely sober by the time he heard his wife and the two young people returning, shortly before lunch time. They were laughing and in high spirits. Richard stood and stretched, and made for the hallway. Antonia's face had an attractive, healthy outdoors glow, as did that of his son. Richard registered on one level what a fine couple they made. Helen too was in a good humour: riding always improved her demeanour.

Perhaps part of Helen's good humour was not due to the rather enjoyable ride the three of them had had, but to the knowledge that she had thrust Antonia in the way of her son, thus depriving her husband of the young English woman's company for the morning.

'You had a good time, I see,' Richard remarked to Antonia, almost sulkily.

'Oh yes! It was fun!' She smiled at Jeremy, who grinned back at her. Richard ground his teeth.

But by the second week of August (with the days growing noticeably longer now), Jeremy had been back at school for a while. With his absence (other than the occasional weekend visit home), a certain degree of edgy, uneasy pleasure at his company had been removed from Antonia's days, and she was able to relax once again into the comfortable, exclusive relationship she had with Richard (for Antonia had no relationship to speak of with Helen, and often only saw her over breakfast).

On Wednesday evening the 11th August, Richard, Helen, Antonia, and most of the hotel's residents, were watching the television in the residents' lounge (which in Richard's great-aunt's day had been the drawing room). Richard (who had had several drinks already that evening) held a large whiskey; Helen was drinking a glass of Cape white wine and smoking one of the Sobranie Cocktail cigarettes she permitted herself in the evening; Antonia, and some of the residents, were drinking tea or coffee. Only Mr. Carstairs had joined the Channings in a drink – in his case, a South African medium cream sherry. Richard rarely bothered to watch television, but a number of Helen's friends had been telephoning her during the late afternoon to talk excitedly about the various rumours of rioting in black townships outside Cape Town that day, and Helen had communicated these rumours to her husband. For everyone at Pitlochry House, the first they really knew of how serious the rioting in the black townships had been that day, had been while watching scenes of the day's violence on the television news. Several black rioters had been killed by the police, and unrest had spread across the Cape Flats. (It was later established that there had been at least seventeen black fatalities through police action).

The television camera panned across scenes of arson and destruction; of wrecked and burned out vehicles, and streets liberally strewn with the rocks, bricks and stones thrown at the police by the rioters.

After this distressing, even shocking, news broadcast (which some of the old ladies absorbed, however, without the least visible reaction, while others began shocked conversations with their immediate neighbours), Antonia turned to Richard and asked, 'Is this going to get worse, do you think?'

'I honestly don't know,' answered Richard. 'But I don't think the country will come out of this unchanged. I think that black anger against the Apartheid regime has been building up for a long time.'

The National Party had been in power without a break in South Africa since 1948. Many segregationist laws had already been passed before they gained power, but during their grip on political life in South Africa, the political philosophy and institutional system known as "Apartheid" had been perfected.

'Are the Coloured people as angry as the blacks are?' Antonia asked Richard.

'I don't think so,' he replied. 'I do not think the Cape Coloureds suffer as much under Apartheid as the blacks do. In fact, in a sense, Apartheid protects them from black dominance.'

That night, as they were preparing for bed, Richard said to Helen, 'So, do you still think this is all going to blow over?'

Helen did not answer, but glared at him. In truth, she had begun to feel a little anxious for the future.

Almost every evening, the television news broadcasts now showed large bodies of black marchers and demonstrators, usually in and around Johannesburg, but sometimes at other points around the country, accompanied by images of destruction, in particular, of burned out vehicles. Almost always, these demonstrations and marches ended in riot and violent confrontations with the police, invariably with yet more fatalities accruing to the demonstrators.

Chapter Seven

On Wednesday morning the 1st September, Richard, accompanied by Antonia, had been shopping in Cape Town for some kitchenware which Elsbet the Cook had said was urgently needed for the hotel. As they exited a well known department store in Adderley Street (having arranged for their purchases to be delivered to Pitlochry House Hotel by Friday), they heard distant waves of angry sound, almost like a heavy surf breaking on the shore. At first the sounds came from far further down the street, but the noise was growing closer even as they stood there on the pavement. Others too had heard the troubling sounds, and a small group was gathering on the pavement outside the entrance to the store. Then Richard heard the sound of police sirens drawing rapidly towards them from further up Adderley Street, and numerous police vans began to pull up alongside the pavement, the noise made by their sirens fading away The doors of the vans were flung open, and several score of police officers, armed with what appeared to be pump action shotguns, leapt out and took up position across the dual lanes of Adderley Street, and some distance down the street either side. Richard could not yet see the marchers, although the sound they made, surging and angry, reminded him more than ever of the sound of a heavy surf on Long Beach after a storm, but he guessed that the demonstrators were using Adderley Street as their route towards the heart of the city centre. He stood and waited, curious to find out what would happen next. The gathering of bystanders (almost all of them Europeans) had grown larger, and the group was charged with an electric field of nervous excitement, and many of its members were talking loudly to one another, craning their necks to try to see what was happening further down the street. Then an SABC TV camera crew arrived, and began filming the occasion. One of the cameras panned across the group of people outside the store.

'What do you think is happening, Richard?' Antonia asked.

'I don't know. I hope there wont be violence.'

The waves of angry sound could now be made out as a rhythmic chanting, and Richard, whose superior height allowed him to see over the heads of the crowd gathered on the pavement, could see the marchers, all of them black, most of them young men. The march came to a ragged halt, perhaps sixty or seventy feet from the police line, and its members began to stamp their feet from side to side, their bodies swaying, chanting in unison, performing that collective dance – a deeply disturbing sight, Richard thought – that would soon become known as the "Toyi-Toyi." Then a command rang out in the police line, and the policemen (all of them Europeans) raised their shotguns to their shoulders, aiming high. Another command followed, and there was an explosive crash of sound as the police fired in unison, and the air was suddenly filled with drifting smoke. A woman in the crowd screamed. Richard could smell the tang of cordite.

Antonia flinched and grabbed Richard's arm.

'I think we should leave!' Richard exclaimed. Holding Antonia close to him, he shoved his way through the crowd, which was suddenly beginning to break up as others arrived at his decision. He was glad that they were unencumbered by shopping. Walking rapidly, Antonia clinging to his arm, Richard made his way up Adderley Street, fearful of being trapped in a situation of violent confrontation. Even as the angry yelling of the mob began slowly to diminish with distance (the chant had given way to enraged shouts), the pair heard another crash of gunfire behind them.

Richard had parked the car on the Railway Station roof parking, almost opposite the department store he and Antonia had been frequenting. He did not believe that it would be wise to try to reach the car just yet. 'I think we'll get off the street,' he said, and he drew his young cousin into the second of the two well known department stores in Adderley Street, this one some distance further up the street.

Inside the store, where there was a reassuring air of normality, with soothing music playing over the store's sound system, shoppers moving up and down the escalators, pretty objects cunningly displayed in glass fronted showcases, and bright lights shining, Antonia said, 'I was scared, out there.'

Antonia's shocked, wide eyed expression excited in Richard a powerful protective urge. 'I was rather anxious too,' he responded. 'No doubt we'll see some coverage on the television this evening.'

Richard and Antonia spent about forty-five minutes in the department store's restaurant, where they had an early lunch: a vegetable consommé for starters, with a chicken curry to follow, and a piece of sponge cake each with custard for dessert. By this time of day, what Richard really needed was a drink (even more so today, in light of their recent experience), but the store's restaurant did not have a liquor licence. As they drank a second cup of coffee each, Richard said, 'The demonstration, or whatever it was, is probably long over by now. The police looked as if they meant business. I think we'll go get a drink at Jamie's.'

'Who is Jamie?'

'The Jameson Tavern – Cape Town's oldest bar,' Richard replied. 'It's full of character. It's where I usually have a drink when I'm in Town.'

As they walked down Adderley Street again, towards the pedestrian crossing to the Station, opposite the department store they had first visited, all was quiet. It was clear that the demonstration was over. Although some police vans were still parked opposite the department store, there was no sign of the black marchers – and nor, happily, was there any sign of bodies.

'It looks as if for once there may have been no fatalities,' Richard commented.

The pair crossed the dual carriageway, which was littered with empty shotgun cartridges, bright red and capped with shining brass, and made their way to the car, parked on the Station's flat roof.

'At a pinch we could walk to the Jameson Tavern. It's in Buitenkant Street,' Richard remarked, 'but it's a fair distance. We'll take the car.'

Richard drove down Newmarket Street, then he turned right into Buitenkant Street, and Antonia noticed a mighty stone bastion on her left, set back some distance from the road. 'Oh!' she exclaimed. 'That must be Cape Town Castle.'

'Yes, it is.'

They passed a stretch of high stone wall, built with a slight inward slope, then another angular bastion appeared.

'We'll visit the Castle sometime, if you like,' Richard said.

'I would enjoy that,' Antonia answered.

The Jameson Tavern was located in a high ceilinged, single story building of no great size, and of plain appearance, alongside which was a lower extension. The walls of both were whitewashed, the windows and doors trimmed in green. To Richard's knowledgeable eye it was clear that the buildings had been modelled on early nineteenth century Cape Town town houses – indeed, this had probably been their original function. There was a small, open, paved area in front of the Tavern for a few tables to be set up during the summer, where drinkers could sit outside. Inside, the high ceilinged room seemed rather dark, and Antonia imagined that it was pleasantly cool in summer. She could just make out framed prints and watercolours hanging on the walls. On later examination, these proved to be urban and landscape scenes of Cape Town and the Cape Peninsula. Antonia thought she had seen many pubs in England with far more character, but she supposed it felt different in the evenings. Of course, "character" in such venues is made up of happy associations, of recollections of convivial drinking with friends, rather than of inert architectural or decorative features. Antonia, unlike Richard, had no such memories of the Jameson Tavern to draw upon, and therefore the pub seemed to her to be somewhat bereft of character. The interior did however possess a certain pleasing simplicity, Antonia thought. There was just a scattering of customers, almost all of them middle aged men.

'It's a lot busier in the summer,' Richard said, perhaps aware that there did not, after all, appear to be anything very special about Jamie's today. 'They serve real ales here, if you would like to try one. Or would you prefer a Cinzano and lemonade?'

'Actually, I think I'll have a scotch and soda, please, Richard.'

Richard, however, was after an Irish whiskey. They took their drinks to a bare, scrubbed wooden table. Richard had obtained a single scotch and soda for his young cousin, and a large, neat Jamesons for himself. (They were temporarily out of Bushmills, his usual choice, so he was told). As far as Richard knew, the pub's name had nothing to do with Jameson's Irish whiskey.

'Cheers,' he said, and gulped at his whiskey.

'Cheers,' Antonia responded, and sipped at her scotch and soda. Then she reached across and touched Richard's hand. 'This is a good idea, Richard. I still feel rather shaken after those scenes we saw. Those black demonstrators – they seemed to have left their individual humanity behind.'

'That's the nature of a mob,' Richard responded. 'That's

why mobs are so dangerous. The police were right to break it up before those people went on the rampage.'

'Do you think they might have gone on the rampage?'

'Yes. I've lived in Africa long enough to know what black mobs are capable of.'

'And white mobs also,' Antonia responded, removing her fingers from Richard's hand.

'No doubt – it's just that we don't tend to get white mobs out here.'

Antonia had a young middle class English woman's rather liberal outlook, and she felt some sympathy for people of colour in South Africa – and yet (she thought to herself) the sight and sound of that dehumanised crowd of demonstrators, stamping their feet and chanting and swaying in unison, had scared her.

'I think I needed this whiskey,' she remarked, taking another sip, then another.

'I think I'll have one more,' Richard said, for he had quickly dispatched his large Irish whiskey. 'May I get you another drink?'

Antonia smiled. 'OK, another scotch and soda, please,' she replied.

'Right-O …' and Richard got up from the table and made his way to the bar counter.

Helen had spent the afternoon at the Van Der Poels' house in Noordhoek, in Charles Van Der Poel's company. She had told her husband that she would be spending that night with her friend, Sonia Van Der Poel, but Sonia was away in Somerset West, and she would not be back home until the next morning.

When Richard heard from Helen that she would be spending the night at the Van Der Poels, he experienced a momentary qualm, almost instantly forgotten. In fact, his instincts had cut in, but the message they were transmitting was not noted. And so, Helen had Charles Van Der Poel to herself all afternoon and all that night to come.

Sonia's husband was besotted with Helen's trim, athletic body, for his wife, always inclined to chunkiness, had put on even more weight recently. Helen, in her somewhat passionless, clinical fashion, revelled in the sex she had with Charles, who was a big, jowly, somewhat coarse and very wealthy man. That the sex was forbidden, irregular, gave it a piquancy that she had never known with sex with Richard – even in the early days of their marriage.

When Richard and Antonia returned to Pitlochry House around half past three that afternoon, Richard, knowing that he would not be seeing his wife until the following morning at the earliest, was in a holiday mood. Perhaps because they had witnessed no actual violence, the confrontation they had observed in Adderley Street earlier that day had not made the same deep impression on Richard that it had made on his cousin. Antonia however still felt disturbed by what she had witnessed; by the imminence of violence (even if not fully realised), by the images she retained in her memory of a large body of people stripped of their individual humanity. She had felt the potential threat they had embodied. She had felt afraid.

Richard remembered how Antonia had clutched at his arm for reassurance outside the department store, and how she had kept hold of him thereafter: there had been little evidence then of the confident, independent and self assured young woman that Antonia had at first seemed to Richard to be; there had been only a frightened girl, looking to him for protection. Richard had felt deeply moved by Antonia's trust in him, by his discovery of the girl beneath the self assured veneer.

What a lovely young woman she was!

Richard was finding that Antonia was more and more often in his thoughts. He found himself thinking of her at all sorts of odd moments. Taking Katy for a short walk on the mountainside, in the last of the daylight, alone but for the dog, he was conscious of the view to the west: that vast vista of ocean. A band of tangerine light rimmed the far horizon, and the underside of the bank of dark cloud above the horizon was touched by a peach blush. It was a sublime view, which should (Richard knew) have raised his mind from base concerns, yet he could not stop himself from thinking about Antonia: her arm in his, her fingers on his hand, her shining eyes, her frightened, trusting little face …

Then his sly and hurtful mind threw a spanner in the works of his pleasant day dreaming. Oh God, he thought: my bloody marriage … !

Chapter Eight

The next morning, Helen returned from her afternoon, evening and night of illicit pleasure, to be greeted rapturously by Skattie, her little Skippertjie dog. ('Skattie my darling! Are you glad to see Mummy home, then?') Skattie was very glad to have her mistress home again, and to be made a fuss of, for during the night, Richard had shoved the little animal unceremoniously from the bed when it had jumped up onto it.

Judging that perhaps he held some moral advantage over his wife (although unaware of just how much of a moral advantage he held over Helen right now), Richard prevailed upon her to permit Antonia and himself to take two of her horses out for a ride. Helen, touched perhaps by some small residual sense of guilt at her adulterous excesses, acceded to Richard's request without argument. Richard was surprised: although it was he who paid for the upkeep of Helen's horses, she was fond of imagining that the small sums of her own money she periodically spent on them constituted the entirety of the financial outlay her expensive equestrian pastime required. (Charles Van Der Poel's business manager submitted Richard a quarterly invoice for stabling charges, an invoice Charles himself never referred to, and it was Richard who paid for the horses' feed, along with periodic visits from the veterinary surgeon – and of course, the animals' shoeing by the blacksmith).

Rather taken by surprise then at Helen's readiness to comply with his request, Richard expressed his gratitude with more than bare civility. 'Thanks, Helen. I thought we would ride out on Long Beach.'

'I'm sure the girl will enjoy that,' Helen remarked. 'We did not visit Long Beach together. Just don't exhaust the horses with too long a gallop on the beach, will you?'

'Of course not! I'm not sure that Antonia is even up to a gallop.'

'Actually,' said Helen, 'she's quite a good rider. Jeremy was impressed.'

Long Beach extended from the foot of Chapman's Peak in the north to the tiny seaside community of Kommetjie, which lay about five miles to the south. The Atlantic Ocean washed against the Cape Peninsula's western shore, and on a rough winter's night, Richard had sometimes heard – from his eyrie high up on the mountainside – the mighty storm-driven Atlantic rollers crashing upon Long Beach with a deep booming sound. But on this morning, the weather was unusually clement (although winter was not yet past). There was a light breeze, and the sun kept breaking through the cloud. The tide was going out, and the surf broke some distance out, lapping upon a damp strand. Sea wrack and long-stemmed kelp seaweed (there were stems over fifty feet in length, which were as wide through as a man's thigh) lay revealed upon the shore. Whitefronted Plovers, along with the ubiquitous Kelp Gulls, were scavenging the ever retreating shoreline. Still damp, but firming sand, made an ideal surface upon which to ride. Richard and Antonia could see no sign of any other Human activity on the beach, no footprints or hoof prints in the sand: they were alone, but for their mounts.

'We could be all alone on a desert shore,' Antonia commented. 'The first people ever to see this beach.'

Richard found her whimsy appealing. He smiled. 'I don't think we're going to come across our Man Friday, though,' he said. Antonia laughed, her eyes shining.

The pair of them had not got above a trot on their way to the beach from the Van Der Poel stables (where they had come across neither Sonia nor Charles, but had dealt with one of the Coloured stable hands). They rode past scattered dwellings, livery stables and small farms, and Richard observed Antonia discreetly as she rode: her back was straight but supple; she rose easily in her saddle; she had an excellent seat. Having decided that she was indeed a competent rider, Richard suggested on reaching the beach that they canter. Wordlessly, the young woman applied her heels to her mount, and the horse leapt forward. Antonia realised that, given the chance, the animal would happily gallop, but she reined it in to a canter, and looked over her shoulder, smiling.

'Come on then!'

Richard was two or three lengths behind her to begin with, and the two animals cantered along the shoreline, Antonia maintaining her lead. Occasionally, the horses would pound through the retreating surf, and the spray, flung high by their hooves, and glistening in the bright light, would soak their riders' legs. Antonia laughed with simple pleasure, and Richard thought that he must surely be in love with her. What a girl!

'How about a gallop!' Richard shouted, coming abreast of her, and Antonia lent forward in her saddle, crouched low, and urged the willing animal into a full gallop. Richard, alongside her, whooped for sheer pleasure. His horse, a powerful seventeen hands grey gelding (the same mount his son favoured when he went riding), soon overtook Antonia (who was riding a fifteen hands chestnut mare, Helen's favourite mount), and as he passed her, Richard grinned at her, and once again she laughed with pleasure and happiness.

After a quater mile or so at a full gallop along the empty beach, both riders eased their mounts back to a canter, then a trot, and then reined in to a halt, grinning at each other.

'That was fun!' Antonia declared. Her face was flushed with exertion and excitement.

'Yes, it was. I don't ride often enough anymore. Where did you learn to ride so well, Antonia?'

'We had horses at home,' Richard's young cousin answered. 'I cannot remember a time when I wasn't able to ride.'

'We had horses at home too,' Richard responded.

'Where did you grow up, Richard?' Antonia asked him.

'In Oxfordshire, on the edge of the Cotswolds. But of course, I was away at school a lot of the time. What about you?'

'Gloucestershire,' Antonia answered. 'But you must have been a very young man when you came out to Cape Town.'

'Yes, I was,' Richard replied. 'I was only twenty-one. My great-aunt, who owned Pitlochry House, kept horses in the stables behind the house – where the garages are now – so I kept up my riding for a while.'

'And of course Helen and Jeremy ride,' Antonia remarked.

'Yes.' Richard frowned momentarily, then, his face clearing, he said, 'There's an old wreck further on. Shall we go look at it?'

'OK.'

The pair kept their horses to a walk for a while, then they broke into a trot, and then once again, a canter. It was not long before Antonia saw the dark silhouette of some large object in the sand.

'Is that the wreck?' she asked.

'Yes, the Kakapo. It grounded on the beach in 1900.'

All that now remained of the small cargo ship was its huge scotch boiler, along with the stern post – with the remains of the rudder still attached – and a row of iron ribs protruding from the sand either side.

'How did the wreck come about?' Antonia asked, walking her horse along the length of the poignant remains.

Richard, keeping pace with her, replied, 'The ship was on its way from England to Australia. They had called at Cape Town, then they continued south. As they reached Chapman's Bay they thought they had rounded Cape Point, and put the helm over to port – and ran aground. I believe there were attempts to refloat the vessel, but as you see, they never succeeded.'

That Thursday afternoon the 2nd September, Helen went shopping in Cape Town. There was nothing she really needed:

she was simply feeling bored, and shopping was her chief leisure pursuit (although riding, and idle afternoon games of bridge with her equally idle friends, were close seconds). She had just exited a jeweller's near the corner of Strand and Adderley Streets, having purchased a pair of jade earrings in a gold setting (a bargain at one hundred and sixty Rand!), when she became aware that she was hearing rising and falling waves of sound drawing near. As she stood outside the shop, uncertain of her next move, having just decided that what she was hearing was massed chanting, wailing sirens drew rapidly nearer, and more than half a dozen police vans came to a halt up and down the street, their tyres screeching on the road. Avid for drama (despite her instincts, which were advocating caution and retreat), she walked to the corner of Strand and Adderley Streets: a mass of policemen had gathered just a short way further down Strand Street, just across from its intersection with Adderley Street. As she watched – just one among a growing crowd of bystanders now – the police marshalled themselves across the road and down either side of Strand Street. They were all gazing to the east – this was one of the main arteries in and out of Town – and from that direction the chanting grew louder and louder. Then Helen could see the first of the marchers appear, a great mass of them – young Coloured men, for the most part. Caution at last kicking in, she began to retreat, but this was not very easy: the crowd around her had grown.

Behind her, as she pushed her way back through the crowd, she could hear the chanting, very loud now, interspersed with individual shouts of anger and rage, and she heard the series of barked commands among the police force. She began to feel the imminence of panic, and pushed her way through the crowd with grim determination, trying to hang onto the two shopping parcels she was carrying. The sound of gunfire behind her made her gasp. Now she did panic, and she dropped her shopping on the ground, and the crowd began to break up around her. There came the shocking sound of further gunshots behind her. A bitter, sharp tang could be felt, as much as smelled, in the air, and Helen realised immediately that it was teargas, although she had never experienced teargas before. People now began to run down Strand Street, heading west, holding handkerchiefs (if they had them) over their mouths and noses. Helen was overtaken by many of them, for she was wearing smart high-heeled shoes, which were not conducive to running. By the time she reached her car, where she had parked it in Bree Street, her eyes were streaming and she was sobbing.

However, the air was clearer here, and once she was sitting in her car, she began to feel calmer, and she dabbed at her eyes and blew her nose several times with a pretty, embroidered little handkerchief she had in her handbag (which, unlike her shopping bags, she had managed to keep a hold of, for it had been slung over her shoulder). She was able to think clearly again.

Helen had quickly realised that she could not now exit the city as usual via Strand Street (and so make her way onto the freeway which connected with Rhodes Drive), not after the mayhem in Strand Street, but she knew Cape Town city centre well: she drove up Bree Street, and turned left into Roeland Street, which she followed south-east, thus gaining access directly to Rhodes Drive. It was with enormous relief that she now headed away from the city along Rhodes Drive, skirting the flanks first of Devil's Peak, and then the eastern slopes of the Back Table, and so, in due course, reaching the Simon Van Der Stel Freeway to the south.

Helen arrived at Pitlochry House as the two maids were clearing away the tea things. Ignoring the greetings of Mrs. Stoddart, who was stationed behind the reception desk, and of Miss Grogan, who was making for the staircase, Helen rushed for the bar in the corner of the great hall. Several of the residents were still sitting in this enormous room, and Helen waved absently as one or two called out a greeting to her. Helen had only one objective in mind: a very stiff drink. Only once she had poured herself a large brandy, and drained the contents in two gulps, did she begin to feel less shattered by recent events. She was pouring herself a second brandy when André arrived, to begin his evening shift behind the bar.

'Madam – ! You look shaken. Are you alright?' he asked.

'Oh, André, you wouldn't believe what I've been through in Cape Town this afternoon. I'm going upstairs to our private sitting room, if anyone needs me.'

So saying, and clutching the second glass of brandy in one hand, her handbag still slung over one shoulder (how fortunate that she had placed her new jade and gold earrings inside her handbag, for the rest of her shopping was lost), Helen made for the stairs. There was a telephone in their private sitting room, and Helen sat down next to it. As she took a few sips from her glass, she dialled Sonia Van Der Poel's number.

By what convoluted mental processes did Helen continue to regard Sonia as her best friend and closest confidante, when Helen was betraying her friend as frequently as she could, via her adulterous affair with Sonia's husband? It is doubtful that even Helen could have answered that question. No matter, Helen was bursting to recount her adventure to someone: the thought of trying to find her husband never crossed her mind. Anyway, she wasn't even sure he was around right now.

Richard, however, was in his office, accompanied by Katy, who was curled up in her bed. Earlier that afternoon he had been on the telephone to the agency he used in Cape Town, to book some bands and country and folk singers for the few remaining Friday and Saturday nights of the winter season. During the summer season – from early October until mid-May – there would be no more live music at the Pitlochry House Hotel. Then, after tea with Antonia in the great hall, where he had greeted several guests cheerily (as he was still in rather a good mood – a consequence of his bracing ride with his young relation that morning – and was feeling fairly sober), he had returned to his office (leaving Antonia writing letters in the residents' lounge), where he read a few more pages from E.M. Forster's novel, *"A Passage to India,"* set in India in the 1920s. Richard's literary tastes – such as they were (he was not usually a great reader of fiction) – were catholic, but he enjoyed reading about life in India during the days of the Raj. As a boy he had been particularly fond of listening to his paternal grandmother tell him stories of the family's time in India during the early years of the century. Richard's grandfather had been fairly senior in the ICS (the colonial Indian Civil Service), and his grandparents had lived in some style. Richard's father had, in fact, been born in India.

Richard had once read more non-fiction than fiction. Increasingly, however, the sheer escapism that fiction offered him, seemed to match his mood of late. Nonetheless, when he bought himself a book, it was still more likely to be about the fauna and flora of the Western Cape, or the history of Cape Town. He was also interested in Cape vernacular architecture (and architecture in general), and maritime lore and marine engineering.

Despite Richard's sense that he would probably not have liked E. M. Forster as a man, the story had nonetheless begun to grip his imagination. Doubtless the setting appealed to him: that of a pre-independence India; an India his father and grandparents would have found familiar. Richard had begun reading the novel quite by chance, finding it amidst a stack of forgotten books in the deeper recesses of a neglected cupboard in his office. In fact, Richard was not to pick the novel up again after today. However, for now, he sat reading in the comfortable leather armchair in his office, sipping from a glass of Irish whiskey, a cigarette in one hand.

Just before six o' clock, Richard turned on the wireless set, which dated from the late 1940s, and was housed in a domed mahogany cabinet. Thus it was that he learned there had been a second serious disturbance in Cape Town, only the day after he and Antonia had witnessed the earlier event. On this occasion, the police had, it was reported, resorted not only to firing birdshot at the demonstrators, but teargas also. There were no fatalities reported – as yet. Richard now thought he remembered something that Helen might have mentioned over breakfast – about her intention of going shopping in Cape Town this afternoon.

"I had better make sure she's OK," he thought to himself, and he put his glass of whiskey down and left the office, Katy at his heels. In the entrance hall, Richard learned from Mrs. Stoddart that Helen had returned home soon after tea time, seemingly well, although somewhat flustered, and he decided not to look for her, not very keen to actually find his wife. She was well, Mrs. Stoddart had told him, so he need not feel any further concern for her. He took Katy outside. Beyond the level ground in front of the house, where cars could pull up on the gravel, was a narrow strip of lawn, with a wooden bench on it which needed sanding and re-varnishing. Richard kept meaning to see to it, but there were so many things that needed doing in, on, and around the house. Sometimes he felt overwhelmed by the burden of upkeep of Pitlochry House. It was easier really just to let things slide …

When the house had been built, tons of good bottomland soil had been hauled at enormous expense up the side of the mountain, to make a garden. The lawn was bordered by flowerbeds in which were planted massed cannas and hibiscus, in the fashion that had been popular between the wars. The cannas were already covered in yellow, saffron, pink and scarlet blossoms, while the hibiscus had some early blossoms in pink, in anticipation of the display they would put on from the end of the month. But the gardens were not the house's great feature. Pitlochry House relied upon its imposing Edwardian architecture – its jumbled roofline, its chimneys and gables and attic windows – and above all, on its location high up on the mountainside for its appeal. However, some of the old ladies did enjoy sitting out in the gardens on deckchairs, or on the bench that needed re-varnishing, during the summer.

Richard allowed Katy to do her business on the edge of the lawn. The gardener would in due course get rid of the deposit. The sun had set soon after six o' clock, and the last of the day's light was almost gone, so Richard did not take Katy for her usual walk, but after the dog had performed, the two of them headed for a grove of Mediterranean pines which grew to one side of the house, all twisted and gnarled by the wind, where Katy was able to sniff around in the gloom among the aromatic bed of pine needles, while Richard smoked a cigarette, which he stubbed thoroughly before walking away, for – a lover of the mountains and their fauna and flora – he had a horror, learned early during his stay in the Cape Peninsula, of mountain fires.

Back inside again, it being now fully dark, Richard and Katy found Antonia, who had long finished writing her letters, and was talking to Mr. Carstairs and one of the other residents in the great hall. Richard managed to disengage Antonia from Mr. Carstairs (who, unusually, given her gender, had rather taken to their young visitor from England), and ask her if she would like a drink before dinner.

'Yes please, Richard,' Antonia replied with a smile of greeting. 'A whiskey and soda would be nice.' She reached down and patted Katy's head.

Richard obtained a large Irish whiskey and a whiskey and soda from André, who wished his employer a good evening, and asked after Mrs. Channing. Somewhat surprised at André's interest in Helen's wellbeing, Richard replied, 'She's well, as far as I know.'

'Madam looked shaken when she got home this afternoon,' the barman continued, 'and I hear there has been trouble in Cape Town again today.'

Richard was not particularly concerned for his wife's welfare. She was home, in one piece. He would doubtless learn more later. He returned to Antonia, who was sitting near the fire. He handed her the whiskey and soda, and sat down himself. 'Cheers,' he said, raising his glass to her.

'Cheers,' Antonia responded.

'So, I heard on the wireless that there's been more trouble in Cape Town today,' Richard remarked.

'Yes, we've just been watching the report on the TV news,' Antonia replied. 'That's two days in a row. And it seemed worse than yesterday's events.'

'I hope you don't regret visiting Cape Town now,' Richard said, smiling at his young cousin.

'Of course not,' Antonia responded. 'What worries me, though, is that the news on the TV in England will be making a big drama of all this, and my family may be worried for me.'

'We can telephone them, if you want, Antonia,' Richard said.

Antonia smiled. 'That's kind of you, Richard. But if they're really concerned, they can always phone us. Do you think things will calm down soon?'

Richard frowned. 'I'm afraid they might grow a lot worse.'

'Oh, I hope not. I have already grown to love the Cape. It's horrible, to think of troubles like this in Cape Town.'

'I know what we'll do, I shall take you to lunch at the

seafood restaurant in Hout Bay tomorrow,' Richard declared, 'and we can forget our anxieties.'

'While eating delicious seafood! I would enjoy that very much, Richard.'

In a short while, dinner was served. Richard and Antonia took their drinks through to the dining room. There was a buzz of more than usually animated conversation at the big table at which the residents were seated: most of them had been watching the news broadcast on the television. At the table for four at which Richard sat with Antonia and his wife, Helen recounted in considerable detail her adventure in Cape Town that afternoon.

'It was awful, dreadful!' Helen told them. 'My eyes were streaming from the teargas by the time I managed to get away.'

'You poor thing,' Antonia responded. 'It must have been horrible. But you did not actually see the police shooting?'

'No – I was trying to escape the scene by the time I heard the first shots.'

'Well, I'm sure we're all glad to see you safe now,' Antonia commented, her expression suitably earnest. Richard said nothing at all. But over pudding (Roly-Poly, with chocolate spread inside, instead of jam), Richard remarked, 'It might be wise to avoid going to Cape Town for a while, Helen.' (And that might stop you spending my money!)

But Helen seemed to think that Richard might have a point. 'Yes,' she agreed, 'I don't think I shall visit Town again until all these troubles have blown over.' She stared at her husband, her face expressionless. 'After all,' she continued, 'there are some excellent shops in Rondebosch and Claremont.'

Helen's Skippertjie dog (which, unlike Katy, enjoyed unimpeded access to the dining room during mealtimes) yapped once, as if in agreement with its mistress. Richard made a small grimace.

'What a lovely pudding,' Antonia remarked to Helen. She felt sorry for Richard. She herself did not like Helen very much (although she was careful to be pleasant to her hostess, thus her choosing to compliment Helen on the delicious pudding), and she had long ago realised that Helen was not at all fond of Richard.

Richard deserved better! "He needs someone to love him," thought Antonia.

Chapter Nine

Antonia had met Toby at a hunt ball late last year. She had been only seventeen years old then, having left school earlier that year, and Toby, who was (she thought) breathtakingly good looking, was then nineteen. He was a local farmer's son, and although his family's social ranking was some way below that of the Binghams, and he had only a moderate education from the local state school, his good looks, his confidence and his charm won him friends wherever he went. When Antonia had met him, he had been looking for amusement and diversion. What could be more amusing than toying with the affections of a piece of (as contemporary cant would have it) "posh totty"? And so he played with Antonia's affections, maintaining at least one other amorous relationship even as he swore to Antonia that she was the only girl for him. He was, in short, a cad. Or, as Antonia had had occasion to call him (on discovering him almost entirely naked in his father's barn one early summer's evening with a girl in similar *déshabillé*), a shit.

Antonia had been devastated. She had never before loved a boy so passionately, or allowed a boy such liberties with her person. She could not believe she would ever love another boy as much. But Richard was not a boy: he was a mature man, and still very good looking (or so Antonia thought). She was not blind to the fact that Richard was bowled over by her. She had never before been the recipient of such obsessive interest from a member of the opposite sex. (There had of course been the usual schoolgirl crushes at her boarding school, in which she had been both infatuant and infatuee, but in either case, these hot house relationships with other girls had rarely lasted more than a term).

Antonia found the experience of being desired by an older man who was as attractive as Richard, rather heady – and wonderful therapy for the hurt caused her by Toby's betrayal of her love.

The morning after Helen's misadventure in Cape Town, there were reports in the two Cape Town newspapers of gangs of Coloured youths committing outrages and acts of vandalism in white suburbs the previous night, including a petrol bomb attack in Fish Hoek, Pitlochry House Hotel's nearest town. Reading these reports, Richard began to wonder how secure Pitlochry House was – isolated as it was halfway up its mountainside, with no near neighbours.

In Richard's office was a gun cabinet, in which were kept three shotguns and a sporting rifle, once the property of his great-uncle, Lord Pitlochry. Richard had not removed them to clean them for years. He could not remember whether there was any ammunition for them. But beneath the gun cabinet were two large drawers: opening them, he found gun cleaning equipment in the first drawer, and in the second drawer, he found several boxes of shotgun shells, but there did not seem to be any ammunition for the rifle. He removed an over-and-under twelve bore shotgun made by Purdey from the cabinet, and broke it, peering down the barrels against the light from the window. He thought there might be some tiny spots of rust in the barrels.

Richard disassembled the shotgun – lock, stock and barrels – and screwed the three-piece wooden cleaning rod together, then attached a phosphor bronze brush which he thought looked about the right diameter to the end of the rod, and ran it up and down the barrels several times. As he recalled, a phosphor bronze cleaning brush would not scratch the barrels. Next, he unscrewed the phosphor bronze brush and attached in its place a woollen cleaning mop, to which he applied some gun oil from a bottle he found with the cleaning equipment. He ran this up and down the barrels a few times. With a yellow duster, he cleaned the choke, and with a soft, oily rag he applied gun oil to it. Next, he applied a drop or two to oil various moving parts, allowing the oil to seep down within the mechanisms. "This is all coming back to me," he was thinking as he worked. Finally, he reassembled the gun, which he replaced in the gun cabinet. "I'll fetch it this evening," he thought to himself. He left a box of shotgun shells on his desk. He was not sure they were even active anymore. Had he ever used one of the shotguns since his arrival at the Cape? He was not sure: he might be confusing himself with a memory which dated from England, for he had used a shotgun occasionally in Oxfordshire. Oh well, he did not think he would really be needing it.

Richard addressed his dog: 'Katy – walkies!' The dog, who had been curled up in her bed in the corner of the office, leapt to her feet, and she and her master left the house, passing the kitchen and domestic offices, and out via the back door. (Richard did not right now feel up to greeting various people in the front of the house). They set off along a path which followed, roughly, a contour line. They walked for a while through a plantation of Scots pines, dark and cool and silent, but before long they came out into bright daylight on the open mountainside. The sandy path was strewn with stones, and occasionally made its way between large outcrops of granite. (Just a little further up the mountainside, the granite gave way to sandstone. The natural spring which fed the small dam just above the house, from which the house drew its water, emerged where water, seeping through the soft sandstone, met hard, impermeable granite). The view was stupendous: in the foreground lay Noordhoek, with its scattered smallholdings, livery stables, farms, and whitewashed dwellings amidst the pines and oak trees (the latter of which were unclothed as yet by the verdant mantle that spring would bring them), and west of Noordhoek were the white sands of Long Beach, bounding the Atlantic Ocean, which was a deep cobalt blue. On a conscious level, Richard was hardly aware of the vista, for he had known it for twenty years now, but even so, he was aware on an unconscious level of the beauty of the setting, and the splendour and tranquillity of the view always succeeded in granting him something of its own spirit, and Richard would return refreshed from a walk along the mountainside with Katy, and feeling calmer than when he set out.

Round about twelve-thirty, Richard found Antonia reading one of the morning newspapers near a window in the great hall. This was Antonia's favourite room, with its high ceiling, its two enormous fireplaces, and its minstrels' gallery, and the dark wooden panelling reaching halfway up the room's height, above which hung a number of oil paintings on the off-white walls. (Whether portraits or landscapes, these were darkened and indistinct now, due to decades of staining by wood smoke from the fireplaces). It was, she considered, such a very English room, owing nothing to the architectural vernacular of the Cape.

Antonia was looking lovely, Richard thought, in a pair of cream slacks and her sweet little green velvet jacket. She had a silk scarf at her throat, and her honey blonde hair, cut in a short bob, shone in the light from the tall window. She smiled and asked Richard whether he had had a good morning.

'The news in the papers isn't very cheerful,' he replied, 'but Katy and I had a good walk.'

'I see there's been trouble in Fish Hoek overnight,' Antonia commented. 'That brings it rather close to home, don't you think?'

'Oh – I don't think we should be worried,' Richard responded. He hoped this was true. He was in fact feeling concerned. If even sleepy little Fish Hoek was no longer safe, how much less secure was Pitlochry House?

But the journey via Chapman's Peak Drive to Hout Bay, the fishing port which lay further up the coast, was as beautiful and dramatic and exciting as Antonia remembered it, and she was feeling an anticipatory, almost childlike, sense of occasion by the time they reached Hout Bay. Richard drove down to the harbour. A moderate southerly breeze was blowing, with white horses dancing in the bay. A dozen or more of the sturdy, beamy, high prowed wooden fishing boats commonly found on either side of the Peninsula were moored on the quayside. Antonia gazed at these workmanlike boats with interest as they walked past them. She could smell mingled aromas of diesel fuel, paint and fish, and beneath these, the fresh briny tang of the sea. There were Kelp Gulls wheeling and screeching in the sky, and scavenging for fish offal in the water below the quayside. The Coloured crewmen working on the boats yelled good naturedly at one another. It was quite a warm day, and most of them were wearing grubby tee-shirts, their arms and faces burned dark by years of sun and weather.

'Oh – look, Richard!' Antonia exclaimed delightedly. 'A seal! Oh, there are more of them!' There were indeed three or four Cape Fur Seals sporting in the water not far from the quayside. Their sleek, wet pelts gleamed as they rolled and cavorted in the water, and their cheeky, sharp snouts made them look alert and aware. 'They're so sweet!' Antonia declared.

'There's a rocky island out in the bay,' Richard told Antonia, 'A seal rookery. They do boat trips there.'

'Can we take a boat trip out there sometime, Richard?' Antonia asked, her tones possessing something of the air of a little girl begging a favour from her father. Antonia was still so young that it was sometimes not clear whether she was treating Richard as a surrogate father or a potential lover – but of this latter possibility, she had little conscious awareness: the amorous signals she sometimes sent Richard were almost as innocent as those an adolescent girl might practice as she explored her femininity; for all her grown up ways, Antonia was, after all, not yet out of her teens.

Richard found Antonia's delighted, girlish enthusiasm most appealing. 'We can do better than that,' he answered her. 'We'll visit Kalk Bay on the other side of the Peninsula. There's a big launch that takes visitors to Seal Island and back. Seal Island is in the middle of False Bay. It's quite a long trip by boat. You don't get seasick, do you?'

'I don't think so,' Antonia replied. 'At least, I've never been any distance in a small boat, but I've never felt sick crossing the Channel by ferry.'

There was a van being loaded with fish laid out in trays of ice, brought in by one of the fishing boats tied alongside the quay. 'We buy our fish here sometimes,' Richard commented. 'But Elsbet and André usually visit the fishmongers in Fish Hoek.'

Antonia, despite her stay at Pitlochry House having extended already for over two months, had never thought to wonder who did the shopping. Come to think of it, she had not seen either Richard or Helen go shopping for provisions in Fish Hoek.

'Does André have a car?'

'Yes, the small Austin van – well, it's actually the hotel's, but André is the only person who drives it. In fact, he's the only member of staff with a driver's licence. He's very useful. He's far more than merely the barman in the evenings and an occasional waiter at meal times. We couldn't get along without him. Either Helen or myself would have to do the shopping for groceries every day otherwise.'

The restaurant was an unassuming structure built of wood, and roofed with corrugated iron, painted blue. Had it not been for the large, painted signboard above the entrance, declaring its name and function, Antonia would have assumed it was some harbour facility. But inside there was a wood-burning stove against one wall, and the restaurant was prettily decorated in a nautical theme. The Cape Crayfish, otherwise known as a Rock Lobster (or *Kreef*, in Afrikaans), that Antonia ate was a treat, absolutely delicious. Richard took pleasure in her energetic enjoyment of the meal. Antonia frequently reminded him how much fun, how vivid life had been, when he had been young. Had Jeremy not closed his father out of his life, Richard would not have needed reminding: he would have shared in his son's enthusiasm for life.

'We both grew up about as far from the coast as it was possible to be in England,' Richard remarked. 'But I could not live away from the sea now.'

'I can understand why,' Antonia responded. 'The beautiful scenery, the delicious seafood.'

'And boats,' Richard added. 'Ships and boats – anything that floats on the sea – exert a fascination for me.'

'You should sail more often,' Antonia said to Richard. 'Jeremy told me you own a yacht at Simon's Town. But you've never mentioned it to me, Richard.'

'You're right. I should get out in the yacht more often. But you know, winter isn't generally the time to go sailing in the Cape. There's the occasional rare day during winter … Perhaps with spring on the way …'

'Does Helen sail at all?'

'No. She has no interest in sailing. With Helen it's horses.' Perhaps, thought Richard, if we had had an interest in common, our marriage might be in better condition today. But he did not voice this thought.

The two of them were back at Pitlochry House by about three o' clock. Antonia went upstairs to powder her nose. Richard, on his way to his office, stopped to greet Mrs. Stoddart behind the reception desk in the entrance hall, and asked her whether there was anything he needed to know. (There was not). Katy was happy to see her master back home, and followed him to the office, where he sat and poured a large Bushmills for himself. He was in fact not entirely sober, although nobody would have guessed this; Richard by this stage of his life had a tremendous tolerance for alcohol. He had drunk the greater part of a bottle of white wine at the seafood restaurant, followed by a couple of liqueurs. (Antonia had had only a glass of wine with her crayfish, and a tiny liqueur at the end of the meal, and the crayfish, and the dessert which followed, had soaked up most of that alcohol).

Richard was now feeling maudlin, and sorry for himself: Antonia had been friendly and lively at the restaurant, but of amorous interest on her part there had been no sign. Sitting at his desk, a cigarette in one hand, a glass of whiskey in the other, he began to experience the sort of anguish that assails some men after they have turned forty, and they come to realise that pretty young women are rarely as interested in them anymore as they once were. (In fact, as a younger married man, although Richard had often flirted with pretty young women, he had never actually been unfaithful to Helen).

But had Richard only known that Antonia (who was by every definition an extremely pretty young woman) at times found him very attractive, he might not have felt that he need mourn the supposed loss of his appeal to the opposite sex.

But did he even have any right, he pondered, to wish for more than Antonia's friendship? Am I in fact in *loco parentis* to her, he asked himself. Is it wicked of me even to entertain a wish for anything more? I'm old enough to be her father!

He groaned. The dog looked up. 'Oh, Katy,' he remarked to the attentive animal, 'I wish it wasn't always so hard!' Katy gave a sympathetic whine, and came and nuzzled Richard's knee. He fondled her face and ears. Poor Richard. He was in a sad way!

Chapter Ten

The news on the television most evenings was full of reports of marches, demonstrations, agitation, unrest, workers' strikes, and localised rioting around the country, with images the viewers were growing accustomed to: large bodies of police, firing into crowds of rioting marchers; burned out vehicles and buildings; streets littered with bricks, stones and small rocks – the missiles flung by rioters at the police – and in many cases, by shoes also, discarded by demonstrators and rioters fleeing police gunfire. The newspapers too were full of reports of unrest and violence. It seemed that news of South Africa's ongoing border war (the previous year, the South African Defence Force had invaded Angola, and come up against Cuban troops) was completely overshadowed by internal events. During this particular evening's news broadcast, Antonia was called away by Mrs. Stoddart, who had answered a telephone call for her from her anxious family in Gloucestershire.

'I'm alright Mummy – *we're* alright, really we are. Things aren't nearly as bad as they appear on the TV,' Antonia assured her mother. Then her father came on the line, and she had to reassure him too. Next: 'No, I don't know when I'll be coming home. I'm having fun here. It's such a beautiful part of the World, too.'

By seven o' clock that evening it was dark, with a last fading glow across the sea in the western sky. Mrs. Stoddart left the hotel in her smart little Volkswagen Golf for her home in Fish Hoek, and soon thereafter, Richard, Helen, Antonia and the hotel's guests sat down to dinner. In a spirit of solidarity in these alarming times, Richard, his wife, and Antonia had abandoned their side table, to sit with the residents at the single long table in the centre of the room. The room was so huge that although brightly lighted directly above the dining table, the corners of the room were in shadow. The tall windows had their heavy velvet curtains drawn against the dark night. There was a constant clatter of cutlery, and an exchange of voices up and down the table. Some voices were louder than others – in particular, that of Miss Chelmsford-Spruce. Mr. Carstairs' fluting tones too were surprisingly carrying. (But then, he had been trained in the theatre to project his voice).

After dinner, two of the guests (including the near-crippled Mrs. Hapgood) retired to their rooms. (There were six long stay residents in the hotel at present, and two short term guests, a German couple in their fifties). Four of the long stay residents, and the German couple, remained downstairs, either in the great hall (where André manned the bar located to one side of the enormous room), or in the residents' lounge, where they watched whatever the South African Broadcasting Corporation had chosen to air that evening on the single channel of television available. Helen and her little dog, Skattie, were upstairs in the Channings' private sitting room; Helen was talking to a friend over the telephone. Richard sat near Antonia in the great hall, nursing a large whiskey, Katy at his feet, his gaze unfocused, while Antonia (who was drinking her second cup of coffee) chatted with the visiting German couple, who spoke excellent English. There was no fire lighted that night; it was not cold enough. Nor were there any casual visitors come for a drink at the hotel that evening; on a weekday evening this was not unusual. No one heard the sound of two cars approaching the hotel on the long driveway up the side of the mountain. The first that the hotel's residents knew of these unwelcome visitors was the almost muted sound of a pane of glass smashing behind a window's velvet curtains. Richard however came to himself with a jerk, and jumped to his feet.

'We've got trouble!' he exclaimed. 'Gather the guests and take them out back to the stables yard, Antonia!' he ordered his young relation. 'Make sure you check the residents' lounge!' Katy let out a bark. Antonia went through to the residents' lounge next door. Richard ran from the great hall, Katy at his heels, through the entrance hall and down the corridor to his office, where he opened the gun cabinet and grabbed the Purdey over-and-under that he had cleaned that morning, breaking it open and loading it with two shotgun cartridges from the box which still lay on his desk. He snapped the gun closed, and stuffed a few more cartridges into his pockets. With Katy following in his footsteps, barking excitedly, Richard ran back to the great hall, the shotgun in one hand, to find that the guests were in a state of confusion, paying little heed to Antonia's efforts to gather them up and lead them to the back door.

'Everyone outside through the back!' Richard ordered them, his voice loud, cutting through the hubbub. 'Quickly now!' There was a hesitant movement among the guests towards the entrance hall.

"I've got to lead them," thought Antonia, "or we'll get nowhere," and in a loud voice she said, 'Follow me!'

Excepting when either Richard or Helen was out in one of the cars, and expected back later that night, the stables court onto which the back door opened was secured at night, the big, sturdy gates to the yard, topped with iron spikes, being closed and bolted from within.

There was another crash of broken glass, which could barely be heard over the babble of alarmed and confused voices, but within seconds, there was a flicker of flame, as one of the heavy velvet curtains caught fire. With frightening rapidity, the flames began to shoot up the curtain, and they speedily jumped to the adjacent curtain across the other side of the window. In the great hall was a fire extinguisher, which was one of several throughout the building. In order to comply with safety regulations, they had been inspected by Fish Hoek Fire Department earlier that year, and Richard (who had placed his shot gun on one of the stuffed and upholstered chairs in the room) seized hold of the heavy fire extinguisher. Resting the base on the floor, he pulled the restraining and arming clip from the top of the device. Aiming the nozzle at the blazing curtains, he depressed the handle, and a jet of thick white foam shot from the muzzle of the fire extinguisher. Behind Richard, the last few of the guests were now making for the entrance hall as fast as they could. For some of them, this was not very fast at all. Only a few of them had any idea how to find their way outside via the back door, but they followed Antonia's lead, as she cried once again, 'Follow me!' and began leading them past the staircase and along the service corridor which gave onto the domestic offices and kitchen and, ultimately, the back door.

André had returned from the entrance hall with a second fire extinguisher, with which he joined Richard in the suppression of the burning curtains. Richard thought he had the fire under control – the flames were out now, and they had not jumped to an adjacent window. But there came another crash of breaking glass, and flames began to flicker at the next window along. Oh God, Richard thought, don't let this device run dry.

André had already begun to direct a jet of foam at the second window, and Richard said, 'I'm phoning for the police and the fire brigade, André! Make sure the fire is out!' He abandoned the fire extinguisher, grabbed his shotgun, and made for the telephone behind the reception desk in the entrance hall.

Richard searched in the front of the telephone directory for the number for the fire brigade, mumbling a litany of, 'Damn-damn-damn-damn,' as he did so. At this moment, Helen appeared at the foot of the staircase, shock written across her face, her Skippertjie dog in her arms.

'Helen! Join the others in the stables court!' Richard commanded her. She left without a word of argument. After what seemed ages, Richard found the number for the fire brigade. It took only a few minutes on the telephone for the

Fish Hoek Fire Brigade to comprehend the nature of the emergency.

'We're on our way, Sir!' they told him. Then Richard rang for the police. Fish Hoek – wonderful, civilised little town – had not only its own fire brigade, but its own police station. A few minutes later, Richard was satisfied that both the fire brigade and the police would be here very soon. He ran to rejoin André in the great hall. He found that André had almost succeeded in putting the fire out on the second window, before his fire extinguisher had ceased working. André, who despite his age was still powerfully built, was shaking it violently. Richard seized hold of the fire extinguisher he had earlier discarded, and aiming it at the smouldering curtains across the second window, he managed to get a weakened jet of foam out of it. It was sufficient to reduce the smouldering remnants of the fire to a nasty, foam covered mess of once thick, heavy velvet material, much of it now on the floor, but some charred and blackened tatters were still hanging from the curtain rails.

Richard picked up his shotgun again, and looking around the great hall, he saw that the enormous space was empty now but for himself, André, and Katy. But it was not yet over: there came another crash of breaking glass, this time, somewhat muted, from the residents' lounge. Richard and André both ran through to the room next door. The television screen still flickered its foolish images of some American sitcom, and canned laughter came from the television's speaker. Thank God, this one was not a petrol bomb. They could see the rock lying on the floor. Richard became aware that Katy was barking.

'Be quiet, Katy!' he commanded the dog. 'Hush!' Katy, good dog, stopped her barking. Richard and André went back through the great hall and checked on the entrance hall; it too was empty.

'André,' Richard said, 'please go check on the folk out back.'

'*Ja*, Mr. Channing.' The Coloured man disappeared past the staircase and headed for the domestic offices and the back door. Only now did Richard become aware that throughout this period there had been shouting outside; angry, brutish sounds, but that it was suddenly silent. He hoped that their attackers had withdrawn, for surely they must have been aware that they could too easily become trapped when the inevitable emergency services arrived. He longed to check on Antonia, but he had to wait here for the arrival of the fire brigade and the police.

The police (armed with pump action shotguns in addition to their usual sidearms) arrived in three vans – more than twenty officers – at almost the same time as the two fire engines did. The hotel's attackers, however, had got clean away, and had been swallowed up by the night before the police had even reached the bottom of the driveway. There was little for the fire brigade to do, other than thoroughly douse the mess of burned out velvet and the scorched wooden panelling either side of the windows, along with the floorboards at the base of the windows. Fortunately the bare, polished floorboards in front of the windows had not been carpeted, and the fire had not taken hold on them, although they had been scorched and blackened.

'If they were locals, we'll find them,' one of the police officers told Richard, 'but they were probably from outside the district.' The European and Cape Coloured communities generally got along fairly well in the Fish Hoek – Kommetjie – Noordhoek district.

By this time, the guests had reappeared from the stables yard, and were gathered in the entrance hall, talking animatedly among themselves. They had been joined by one of the two guests (excluding only Mrs. Hapgood, who remained upstairs) who had earlier gone up to their rooms, and by the servants, who stood in a huddle to one side. Antonia stood with the group of guests, but Helen, her dog still in her arms, had joined Richard. It was after ten o' clock before the emergency services had finally departed. Four fully armed policemen had, however, been left behind at the hotel. Helen organised coffees for them, and two of them made themselves comfortable in the entrance hall, while two found chairs on the veranda. Then Richard said to Antonia and Helen, 'I don't know about you, but I could do with a drink.'

So saying, Richard entered the great hall, which stank horribly of the dampened down detritus of the fires at the windows, and made his way to the bar counter, where he poured his wife a brandy, Antonia and André a scotch (the master-servant relationship had been temporarily suspended), and himself an Irish whiskey. He offered André a cigarette, which the Coloured man took from him, and he lighted himself a cigarette also.

'Give me a cigarette, Richard,' Helen asked.

'Of course.' Helen rarely smoked, and then only Sobranie Cocktails, but this was surely an occasion when a cigarette was needed. She put Skattie down and took the cigarette, which Richard then lighted for her.

'I don't know what I should be feeling now,' Antonia remarked.

'Gratitude,' Richard suggested. 'We thank God – that the fire didn't take hold and spread, and that no one was hurt,'

'Yes – thank God,' Antonia agreed. Helen remained silent. Richard was thinking, "It's going to cost me a fortune to get new velvet curtains, and have the scorched woodwork and floorboards restored …"

He doubted very much that the hotel's insurers would cover the costs of repairing the damage: he imagined that there was an exclusion clause for damage sustained during "riot and insurrection."

Richard finished his whiskey, and poured himself another. 'It could have been far worse,' he remarked. Helen however was making up her mind to go home to her parents in Constantia, on the far side of the mountains, the very next morning. There she would receive the sympathy and doting care which were, she felt, her due, after the recent traumatic events she had had to suffer. She set out in her MGB Roadster, with as much luggage as she could cram into it, and Skattie the dog sitting in the seat next to her, soon after breakfast. She had not told her husband of her plans, and she left without saying goodbye to him.

The German visitors also made their departure.

Chapter Eleven

Aged eighteen, Richard had commenced his studies at Oxford University in October 1953. (His national service had been deferred in order to permit him to study at university. He was in fact never to do his national service, as he went abroad shortly after leaving university). At Oxford, he had played cricket and rugby, and when he and his closest friend at university, Michael Hyde, had graduated in June 1956 (neither young man showed any great academic merit, but both were physically fit and healthy, and each possessed an equable and cheerful nature), they had planned an adventure together: a trans-Africa journey as far as Cape Town. Richard had a great-aunt on his father's side living in some style (his mother had told him) in Cape Town. Michael knew no one in South Africa, but his uncle was farming in Kenya, which lay on their route south.

The two young men had bought a second hand Land Rover for thirty Pounds. This Land Rover would later be known as the Series I. (At the time, the Series II had not yet been introduced). It was the sturdiest, toughest vehicle produced in Britain (if not in the World), and the easiest to locate (or make) spare parts for, across the length of Africa.

'She needs a name,' Michael had declared, as the young men stared at the car, whose somewhat battered body work was painted Land Rover's standard dark green.

'What about Mildred?' Richard suggested.

Michael snorted. 'Mildred! It's not a charwoman, Dickie.'

'I know – there's that jolly, bouncy girl we met last summer, Betty. How about we name the Land Rover Betty?'

'That's much better,' Michael had agreed. 'Betty she is. She needs Christening.'

The two friends had driven together in their Land Rover to a pub not far away, and had spilled a pint of Best on one wing of the vehicle.

'I name thee Betty,' Michael had intoned.

'And may God bless all who ride in her.' Richard had added. Both young men had roared with laughter (they had already enjoyed a couple of pints of Best each). During the next two months, they had found out as much as they could about their proposed route across Africa, a route which would, after leaving Egypt, be taking them entirely through British colonial possessions. Several trips to London, and the Army and Navy Stores, saw them buying the equipment they thought they would need for the journey. They were ready to set off by the end of August. It was a warm, high summer's morning, with the sky above the Oxfordshire countryside an unblemished blue. Birds sang, and Richard's mother, and Katy, his younger sister, saw them off. (Michael had been staying with the Channings at their home in Oxfordshire that summer, and he had made a special trip home to say goodbye to his family in Norfolk a week earlier).

The two friends crossed the Channel by the Dover ferry that evening, arriving at Calais at about nine o' clock. There was still light left in the sky. It took them two and a half days to reach Marseilles. They raised their small tent alongside the Land Rover for each of those two nights, both times near a river or a stream, having bought provisions (speaking their schoolboy French) along the way. After killing time in a cheap *pension* for another three days and nights, they watched while their Land Rover was swung aboard a cargo ship bound for Alexandria. The ship called at Valletta in Malta, and they set foot at last in Africa a week after leaving Marseilles.

'My God, it's warm,' Richard remarked. He removed his hat and mopped his forehead with a large, rather grubby handkerchief. (The two young men had eschewed traditional pith helmets in favour of floppy bush hats, far more practical, in the opinion of the salesman at the Army and Navy Stores in London). The sun was almost directly overhead. The heat, the clamour of noise and activity at the dockside, the Babel of incomprehensible Arabic, the sheer foreignness of the setting, delighted both young men. This was properly "abroad"!

Due to the strict currency regulations then prevailing, the two young men had not been able to leave England with very much Sterling in their pockets. Michael hoped that they might find work, via his uncle, for a while in Kenya, in order to top up their funds. Otherwise, they hoped to find work for a while in Rhodesia. Either way, they were going to be making the journey on very tight purse strings, which was why they had loaded the Land Rover with as much tinned provisions as they could cram into it, after the bulkier items had been packed. These latter included the tent, tools, spare parts for the Land Rover – including a number of leafs for the suspension, as they had heard that a broken leaf spring was one of the most common causes of a breakdown – two five gallon steel jerry cans which would be refilled whenever they might find fresh water, another five gallon jerry can of petrol, a two gallon can of engine oil, kerosene for the lantern, an insulated box for keeping fresh food from spoiling, and two spare tyres and inner tubes (to add to the tyre already attached to the spare wheel mounted atop the bonnet).

It was still September when they crossed the Ugandan border into Kenya. Michael's uncle was busy with the maize harvest. He welcomed the extra labour the two strong young men could provide, but he knew of no regular paying work available. 'The problem,' he said, 'is that the *Watu* do all the labouring work, and there's not much else in Kenya that is open on a short term basis for young white men. But I know the manager of a hotel in Nairobi. Perhaps he could find something for the two of you. I'll give you a letter to present to him.'

So it was that Richard landed up serving behind the hotel bar in the evenings for four weeks, while his friend manned the front desk at night. The hotel manager paid them a pittance – far less than he would have had to pay regular European staff – and was glad of a few weeks of inexpensive work out of the two young men. But even this mean recompense went some way towards topping up their kitty, and in late October the two friends set off again, heading south. (A week later, Britain and Egypt were at war, and Egypt would have been closed to the two young travellers).

The Land Rover proved its worth. The engine had given no trouble, apart from a broken fan belt (and the young men were carrying a couple of spare fan belts), and the only major breakdown had come about when the car had hit a huge pothole, and one of the rear leaf springs had broken. Michael was hugely more gifted at practical mechanics than was Richard, but with Richard's vital assistance (it was a two-man task), he managed to remove the broken leaf spring and replace it with one of the spares they carried.

Both young men were, each in his own way, strongly impressed by the African terrain. For vast distances they came across no sign of Human habitation (Africa's horrifying population explosion lay a long way in the future); not a hint of Man's presence, other than the un-metalled, dusty road itself, and – invariably – the line of telegraph and telephone poles along one side of the road.

Some nights they would put up at a *dak* bungalow,[*] where they could obtain an evening meal (invariably a chicken or goat curry), very basic ablution facilities, and a room in which to lay out their bedding. Other evenings saw

---

[*] "*Dak* bungalow." A rest house and staging post for the mail service, at which travellers could find shelter, rudimentary accommodation, and a meal. *Dak*, from the Hindi for "mail." The term had been used throughout British India, and was still then in use in British East Africa.

them setting up their tent next to the Land Rover, anywhere suitable alongside the road. They had been warned not to make camp near broad, smooth surfaced rivers or wide lakes, for fear of the hippos who would come ashore at night to graze, and crocodiles could be a danger also. They would however periodically empty and refill the jerry cans with water at any free flowing streams they crossed. They would sit in front of their tent, having got a fire going, and listen to Africa's noisy nights. They never grew entirely easy with the maniac giggling of a hyena troop nearby at night, and several times they heard the roar of a lion out hunting no great distance away: great waves of sound, midway between a vibrating grunt and a roar, fading to a deep, repeated coughing. The first time they heard such a sound – not very far away – Michael, whose eyes, gleaming in the firelight, were wide and round, had glanced at his friend. Richard by contrast had a look of deep delight on his face. Michael took comfort in the loaded revolver – which had belonged to Richard's father – that his friend had brought with him.

Of the two friends, it was certainly Richard who gained the greater delight from the African wilderness. The vastness of the land, the heat and dust and long, empty road, the enormous sky above, and at night, the incomparably bright canopy of stars, brighter and far more profuse than anything ever seen in the British night sky, spoke to some deep need Richard had thus far been unaware of.

The two young Englishmen crossed the Limpopo River into the Union of South Africa during the second week of November (and Richard thought of Rudyard Kipling's "great grey-green, greasy Limpopo River, all set about with fever-trees ..." from *The Elephant's Child* in the *Just So Stories*). It was summer time in the southern hemisphere. It took them another four days and three nights to reach Cape Town, and Richard's hospitable great-aunt's magnificent home some distance down the Peninsula. They had spent each of those three nights in a different, but always very similar, municipal caravan and camping site, for almost every *dorp* of any size they passed through on their way south had on its outskirts such a camping site, with shade trees, potable water on tap, barbeque stands and an ablution and lavatory block.

Lady Pitlochry, *née* Lavinia Channing, was the widow of Lord Pitlochry, a Governor of the Union of South Africa during the 1920s. She had chosen to stay on in South Africa after her husband's death in the 1930s, all alone (but for the servants) in the big house on the mountainside above Noordhoek, that she and her husband had bought in the late 1920s. She had, however, many friends in Cape Town society, and she was far from being a recluse. Richard held only unclear memories of her, as he and Michael pulled up in front of the grand old house, their long journey ended: he had been a little boy the last time his great-aunt had visited England. He was now, however, her only living male blood relation, and Lady Pitlochry made much of him – and of his friend, Michael, too.

Lady Pitlochry was then seventy-five years old, a small, elegant woman with a mass of white hair gathered above her head, and her features possessed the fine, patrician bone structure that would permit her to remain beautiful no matter her age.

'Richard,' his great-aunt declared, 'you look so much like your father! He was adventurous, too. It's something in the Channing blood, I think.'

Richard could not remember his father very well, who had died when he was a child.

The two young men took the suburban line from Fish Hoek (which they found was Pitlochry House's nearest town) for Cape Town on a number of occasions, leaving the Land Rover each time in the station car park. They took the Cable Car to the top of Table Mountain – one of the most dramatic short journeys either young man had made. They took the train in the opposite direction also, to Simon's Town, the southern terminus of the Peninsula suburban line, and Richard in particular enjoyed the maritime character of this historic naval base. They explored the Cape Peninsula at large in the Land Rover, and hiked in the mountains that formed a spine through much of the Cape Peninsula. Richard had a Leica camera with him, and he took a great many photographs, which he had developed in Fish Hoek.

Richard's great-aunt was eager that the two young Englishmen meet some youngsters their own age, and she informed her friends of the young men's stay, and Richard found himself invited to several social functions where he met other young people. His great-aunt always made sure that the invitations to these social gatherings included his friend. Michael, like Richard, was a gregarious, sociable young man. The two friends were already having a super time, when Lady Pitlochry announced that she was going to hold a Christmas ball at Pitlochry House. Among the many people she invited were Henry and Maria Du Bois, a well connected old Cape Dutch family, along with their seventeen year old daughter, Helen.

Richard was bowled over by the girl's cool, ethereal beauty. She was, he thought, like some creature out of a fairy tale. Her hair was like the finest spun gold, her eyes a periwinkle blue, her slight figure graceful, elegant, and blessed with a natural poise. Despite an age difference of four years between them (which, while of little account with the passage of time, was significant, given their respective ages, in 1956), Richard hardly left Helen Du Bois alone during the Christmas ball: although she had little to say, when she did speak, her voice – unusually low in a girl so young – captivated him. He could hardly bear to tear his gaze away from this beautiful creature.

Michael however did not take to the Du Bois girl: her fetching but entirely faux little-girl timidity, and her charming air of assumed modesty, left him cold, and in the set of her mouth, he thought he read a hard and selfish individual. And he was correct in thinking that she had been overly spoiled all her life. But his friend was blind to these failings. Nonetheless, Michael did his best, for his friend's sake, to hide his dislike of the girl.

During the course of the next twelve months, Richard and Helen were often together. The Du Bois family was invited to dinners and dances at Pitlochry House, and Richard was invited to barbeques, garden parties and dinners at the Du Bois house in Constantia. As the months went by, Helen's parents would occasionally engineer situations where Richard and their daughter were left alone together (but never in any compromising sense; never, for example, indoors).

Richard and Helen were married fourteen months after their first meeting, in February 1958. (Michael, himself still a bachelor, had visited South Africa again, this time making a sea voyage, to act as best man at his friend's wedding). Helen was eighteen years old, and Richard had just turned twenty-three. The wedding (at the picturesque, stone-built Christ Church in Constantia, the Anglican church where the Du Bois family worshipped) took place despite Richard being at the time employed merely as a part time barman at a pub in Simon's Town, but Helen Du Bois' parents had assumed (correctly, for Lady Pitlochry had intimated as much to Richard) that Richard was Lady Pitlochry's heir, and that he would one day inherit Pitlochry House and his great-aunt's substantial fortune. The newlyweds' three night honeymoon was spent in Hermanus, a seaside resort town within an easy afternoon's drive from Cape Town, and afterwards, Richard brought his bride back to Pitlochry House. Helen soon began to display her essential laziness and self regard, but this meant that she was happy not to challenge Lady Pitlochry for the role of mistress of Pitlochry House. Richard, who was hot blooded himself, was disappointed at Helen's cool, passionless manner in bed, but even so, she managed to bear Richard a son just over a year later, whom they named Jeremy.

Lady Pitlochry died of pancreatic cancer in 1961, aged eighty, and Richard found that he was indeed her heir. He was now the owner of the great house on its mountainside (including the bottom land and the scattering of tenant smallholders that went with it), and the happy possessor of what seemed to the young man to be a sizable fortune. But the fortune was unable to keep up indefinitely with the Channings' expensive lifestyle (a lifestyle driven far more by Helen's desires than by Richard's), and in 1966, in an attempt to stay afloat financially, Richard opened Pitlochry House as a hotel. He had dreams of turning it into a hotel of considerable repute, catering for wealthy foreign guests, and offering five star service and facilities. Alas, Richard no longer possessed a fortune large enough to make his dreams a reality, and the hotel was unable to gain more than two stars, or to escape what soon became its primary function: a residential hotel for elderly long term guests – of whom there were never sufficient numbers for the hotel to do much more than break even financially.

Helen began to wonder whether she had made a serious mistake in marrying Richard, and Richard's drinking began about this time to increase noticeably. Theirs was no longer a marriage made in Heaven

Chapter Twelve

If any of the hotel guests had seen Helen leaving the house after breakfast that morning, her car laden with luggage, with her little black dog by her side, they did not feel it was their place to mention it to Richard. And he did not wonder at her absence at lunchtime: Helen was probably having lunch with a friend somewhere. But when Helen was absent also at dinner time, Richard began to wonder where she was. He asked around, and he learned in due course that she had last been seen driving away from the house soon after breakfast that morning, in a heavily laden car. Richard spent the night alone in bed, which he did not mind: it was a long time since Helen had been any sort of a companion for him. But by mid-morning the next day, a Sunday, Richard thought he had better try to find out where his wife was. So he telephoned her parents, and thus it was that he learned that Helen had left him, and would he mind if Henry and Maria Du Bois drove round in the next few days to pick up the rest of her things?

His first thought was, "I can get a divorce on grounds of malicious desertion, if she keeps this up."

His second thought was, "This gives me a clear run with Antonia."

Richard reached into his desk drawer and withdrew the bottle of Bushmills he kept there, along with a whiskey tumbler, and poured himself a hefty triple shot. Strictly speaking, Richard was rarely fully sober anymore after mid-morning, but if he was (although he refused even to consider such a possibility) an alcoholic, he was at least a functioning alcoholic. He did not (he thought) behave erratically, or make outrageous scenes (his immoderate outburst with the parking warden, when he had collected Antonia at Cape Town Station, had been forgotten), or humiliate himself horribly, all of these the sort of things he remembered an uncle of his doing when Richard was a teenager. The uncle was long dead, the drink having carried him away. Richard did not believe he drank so much that his health was endangered: he was a big man; he could absorb a lot of alcohol.

He gulped the whiskey down with a grimace, in one go. The warmth spread almost instantly through him, as did the feeling of wellbeing. Ahh ... that wonderful first drink of the day!

'Let's go walkies!' he addressed Katy. The dog's tail wagged frantically as she leapt to her feet, and Richard and his dog went to find Antonia, to ask her whether she would like to join them on a walk.

The young woman could not be found. Too bad – he would see her at lunchtime, if not before. Richard had forgotten that Antonia had accompanied Miss Chelmsford-Spruce and Mrs. Hapgood to the Anglican church service in Fish Hoek that morning, all three sharing a taxi which had been sent from Fish Hoek. (The two old ladies went to church in Fish Hoek every Sunday morning, sometimes accompanied by one or two other guests). The hotel had an arrangement with the taxi company, and paid a discounted rate on the fares, billing whichever guest or guests had made use of the taxi service – when Richard remembered to do so. So Richard and Katy set off along the side of the mountain, heading towards the scarp below Silvermine. They were away for more than one and a half hours, returning about half an hour before the gong in the entrance hall sounded for lunch.

Walking on the mountain rekindled memories of happier days for Richard, of a time when he had been young and newly arrived in the Cape, and he had spent a lot of time hiking in the mountains. But this walk was not as calming as most, for during the walk he wondered what he could or should have done better for Helen. He did not understand that his great and unforgivable sin in Helen's eyes was his lack of material success: he was not as rich and successful as most of the men she knew, and he was unlikely now ever to become so. Helen had no wish to shackle herself or her son to someone she regarded as a failure.

After lunch – a traditional Sunday lunch of roast beef with mint sauce and all the trimmings, something the guests always looked forward to (how crisp and golden were the roast potatoes!) – Richard and Antonia took their coffees out to one of the small tables on the veranda. The bite of winter was no longer present, and today it felt quite mild outside. Richard said to Antonia, as the two of them sat down, 'Helen seems to have left me. I learned this morning when I rang her parents.'

'Oh – Richard!' exclaimed Antonia. She was momentarily nonplussed. For all her poise, Antonia was still very young.

'To be honest,' continued Richard, 'I'm not feeling too cut up about it. I suppose it was always going to happen someday.'

'Do you know, has she left for good?'

'God knows. Perhaps she'll be back again. But I expect she would have mentioned something to me had she simply decided to spend a little while with her parents.' Richard laughed. There was a touch of the manic in his laughter, or perhaps it was just the wine. 'You're not thinking of leaving us too, are you – after all the recent excitement?'

Antonia, picking up on Richard's mood, laughed also. 'No, I shant be leaving you yet. But do you think we'll see a repeat of the drama of two nights ago?'

'Probably not,' Richard said, 'but the Fish Hoek Police Chief told me his men would be keeping an eye on us for a few nights.'

'That's good to know.' Antonia looked thoughtful. Then she said, 'Perhaps Helen has just had enough – you know, the scare she had in Cape Town, followed the next night by the attack on the hotel.'

'No, I think she's left me at last.' Richard gulped at his wine. 'I wonder if she will expect me to keep paying for the upkeep of her damn horses?'

'Oh, Richard,' Antonia responded, resting her fingers lightly on the back of his hand. She felt enormous sympathy for him. She knew that he was not without his faults, chief of which was his drinking – but he only drank, she thought, because his wife and son made him so unhappy. 'I expect it will all work out in the end – one way or the other,' she continued. Then she noticed Mr. Carstairs, who had come outside, observing them, and she removed her fingers from Richard's hand.

After the heavy lunch (which had concluded with two enormous spotted dick puddings with lashings of custard), Richard retired to his office for a nap. Antonia was pleased to see that the sun had come out (not that any sunshine could reach the veranda), and she sat in a cushioned cane chair on the veranda and had a short doze. When after half an hour she awoke, she decided to go for a walk. She knew that Richard and Katy would be napping in his office, so she set off alone along the contour trail. "I need to buy some proper walking boots," she thought. "I must mention it to Richard."

The third term of the school year terminated on Friday the 24th September. The boys then had a short holiday, commencing their fourth term (and for Jeremy, his final term at school) on Monday the 4th October. But Jeremy did not come home. Instead (dropping by at Pitlochry House only to collect a few of his clothes), he spent the school holidays at his Du Bois grandparents' home in Constantia, with his mother. Whereas Richard accepted his wife's absence with near perfect equanimity, he felt that of his son keenly. He was afraid that he really had finally lost the boy for good, and the hurt he felt was acute. How had it come to this, he wondered? Jeremy as a little boy had loved his father, and Richard had adored his son. Richard could remember when Jeremy had been born; the nurse bringing him his son to hold, and the overwhelming pride and joy of fatherhood he had felt.

'A son! I have a son!' he had exclaimed. How proud he had been of Helen. How he had loved her too, in that moment.

And now all that huge fund of love was shown to have been a failed investment, a brief few years of joy in a life now beset by disappointment. No wonder Richard clung to the relationship he had with his young cousin from England. It was like a shaft of sunshine in a lowering sky. Although Richard did not fully appreciate just how important it was to his wife that he had failed to have become rich and successful, he knew that she considered that he had failed her in some fashion. But he felt that he had failed his son too – in having alienated his son's love for him. Of all the hurts in his life, this – Jeremy's estrangement from his father – was the greatest that Richard bore. And he felt helpless to address it.

By early October the weather was a good deal warmer, and it was not raining as frequently. The sun shone much of the time, and the oak trees in Noordhoek had exploded in bright, vivid green. Richard was woken in the mornings by birdsong from the oak tree outside the bedroom window. He and Antonia drove to Cape Town one morning in order to buy her a pair of hiking boots (and some thick woollen hiking socks to go with them). They visited the Cape Union Mart in Barrack Street, a venerable camping and outdoors emporium that Richard had known since his early days in Cape Town. How he enjoyed visiting this shop! It was crammed with goods that spoke of happy days outdoors, of mountain hikes, of wilderness adventures. Here they found Antonia a pair of boots by *Lubbe*, the well known bootmakers, and several pairs of thick woollen hiking socks. Richard, who owned a pair of *Lubbe* boots himself, swore by their sturdiness and quality. A South African brand, they had been manufactured in the pretty town of Stellenbosch, not far from Cape Town, since the 1940s.

'Let me pay for the boots, Antonia,' Richard said. 'I want them to be my gift to you, something to help you remember your stay at Pitlochry House.'

'Oh, Richard! You don't have to do that!'

'I want to. And we will go for a proper hike soon. We'll spend a day in the mountains together.'

Antonia smiled and touched Richard's arm. 'I look forward to that,' she said.

After leaving the shop they walked to the Jameson Tavern, which was not far away. It was a beautiful morning: the oak trees which were such a feature of old Cape Town were clothed in bright new leaf; the sky was a clear, pristine blue, with only a light wind blowing. This was not usually a part of Cape Town much visited by tourists, so Richard informed Antonia, although many of the buildings were quite old. 'At least, they're old for Cape Town,' Richard remarked. 'Mid nineteenth century or earlier.' Inside Jamie's (as Antonia recalled Richard referring to the tavern), he asked her whether she would like to have something to eat. 'It's almost lunchtime,' he said.

'I am feeling rather hungry,' Antonia replied. 'You order something for me, Richard.'

Richard examined the menu, and placed an order for some food. He took the Cinzano *Rosso* with lemonade that

Antonia had requested, along with a Castle lager for himself (That's a change, thought Antonia), to their table outside. With the end of winter, tables and chairs had been set up on the paving stones in front of the pub. They were not the only customers seated in the open air: most of the tables outside were occupied. It was close to noon.

'Cheers,' Richard said, raising his glass.

'Cheers,' Antonia responded. After sipping at her drink, she removed her new boots from the box, and placed them on the table in front of her in order to admire them.

'These are beautifully made,' she commented with a smile. 'Thank you.'

'Dear Antonia, you are most welcome,' Richard responded.

'You've been so good to me, Richard,' she continued, and reaching across the table she took his hand. 'I'm so glad I came to visit you.'

'I'm glad too.' Richard and Antonia smiled at each other for a while, then Antonia let go Richard's hand, and he took a deep draught of Castle lager. Antonia was finding that her already warm feelings for Richard had become intensified since Helen's departure. She thought it very wrong of Helen to have left Richard, and cruel of her to have alienated Jeremy's affections for his father – which, as the boy's absence during the recent school break had shown, was clearly what she had done. Antonia felt both compassion and pity for Richard – and some admiration too: he suffered his family's abandonment with fortitude, and showed little self pity. She had come to realise that while she had previously held Richard in the warmest regard, she now felt something very much like love for him. To be sure, he had his fair share of Human frailties, but he was kind and decent – and awfully good looking, too!

A young white woman appeared, with their food on a tray. 'Here's your order, Sir,' she said, smiling, placing a plate in front of each of them. The two stacks of cutlery she also placed on the table were each wrapped in a paper napkin. There were salt and pepper cruets already on the table.

'Thanks,' Richard responded, smiling back at the young woman. "What a pretty girl," he thought.

They set to, but after a minute, Antonia remarked, 'This food is delicious. What is it called? And how is it made?'

'It's called *bobotie*,' Richard answered. He pronounced it "baboaty." 'A traditional Cape Malay dish,' he explained. 'It's made with spiced minced beef or lamb, topped with a baked egg and milk mixture. I'm particularly partial to the juicy dried fruit in the meat. In fact, there are always dried fruits, usually apricots and sultanas, in the curries that Elsbet serves at Pitlochry House. You may have noticed them.'

'Yes, I had noticed. I'd not come across it before. They go very well with a curry.'

'It's the Cape Malay influence on Cape Town's cuisine,' Richard explained.

'I think you have a super menu at Pitlochry House, Richard,' Antonia remarked. 'Nothing too exotic – but plenty of it!'

Richard laughed. 'I try! We cannot offer our guests much, but I believe that if I provide them with good food, I can go a long way to ensuring their loyalty. Dont you agree?'

'Absolutely,' Antonia replied. 'But you know, the actual location of the hotel – that splendid isolation, halfway up a mountainside; the tranquillity and the view – they count for a lot too, I'd say.'

Richard swallowed a mouthful of *bobotie* and sipped at his lager. 'I probably take it for granted,' he said. 'I've been living there for twenty years.' He grinned at Antonia. 'Longer than you've been alive!'

'Oh, Richard! What is one's age, after all?'

'Either a great deal – or nothing at all,' Richard answered. 'Perhaps in matters of the heart, one's age is meaningless.'

The sun shone on the couple, whom some might have mistaken for father and daughter; the pigeons scavenged at their feet for crumbs, and right here, right now, all was (Richard felt) well with the World.

Chapter Thirteen

The Castle of Good Hope is a five bastion, star-shaped fort, built in the seventeenth century by the Dutch East India Company, in order to protect their strategically important Cape of Good Hope way-station on the trading route to the Spice Islands of the Far East. The smooth faced walls built of stone slope slightly inwards, and each bastion commands a wide angle of fire for the canon that were originally mounted atop them. For South Africans (and for visitors to the Castle such as Richard, who admired ancient structures) the Castle was deeply significant, being the oldest surviving building in South Africa, its pentagonal star shape adopted by the South African Defence Force as an emblem.

Richard and Antonia stood in front of the gateway to the Castle, which was surmounted by an elegant bell tower. Richard had suggested, after their lunch at Jamie's (which they followed with a coffee each) , that they visit the ancient structure.

'Oh – yes, I would like that,' Antonia responded. As they walked back to the car in Barrack Street, Richard had explained to Antonia that when the Castle had been built by the Dutch East India Company in the seventeenth century, it had been situated on the coastline of Table Bay, and was then guarded on its landward approaches by a moat fed by the Salt River.

'The Castle was able to protect the settlement from sea-borne attack, as well as an attack by land. Over time, however, a good deal of land was reclaimed from the sea, thus pushing the coastline further and further away from the Castle.'

'That's interesting,' Antonia had responded. 'I must admit,' (she had said with a self deprecating smile), 'I hadn't really wondered why the Castle was located so far from the shoreline.'

Richard laughed good humouredly. 'Well – now you know!'

As they exited the tunnelled entranceway beneath the walls, they saw ahead of them a wide, deep court as big as a parade ground, across the width of which ran a three story building painted in yellow ochre (like all the buildings in the Castle's interior). In the centre of this building was a prominent balcony.

'The balcony you see in the centre of the building is known as De Kat balcony,' Richard told Antonia. 'The authorities would make announcements to the assembled burgers from it.' Richard took Antonia's arm, and turning her around, he said, 'Look at the sculpted pediment above the gateway. It's beautiful, isn't it? It's an example of work by the late eighteenth century architectural sculptor, Anton Anreith, who was famous in the Cape.'

'I never realised you were interested in this sort of thing, Richard,' Antonia remarked with a smile, intrigued to have come across a facet of Richard's character of which she had been entirely unaware. She liked him all the more for it.

'Oh yes – I've always been keen on historical architecture,' Richard responded, his tone of voice enthusiastic. 'Old buildings fascinate me. We have far fewer of them in South Africa, truly old buildings, that is, than you have in Britain; what we do have, are almost all found in and around Cape Town. We have plenty of late nineteenth century architecture, and turn of the century buildings – like Pitlochry House itself.'

Antonia smiled again, and gazed all around her, and even though she had no pronounced interest in the past – certainly, less so than Richard clearly had – the atmosphere of age and history which surrounded them as they stood at the perimeter of the wide parade ground made an impression on her. Cape Town Castle, Richard had told her, was the oldest surviving building in South Africa. Richard had also explained to her that it occupied an important place in the national iconography of South Africa, and was in addition the regimental headquarters of the Cape Town Highlanders.

Antonia was, however, rather taken by the William Fehr collection of paintings and antique furniture housed within this central range of buildings.

'What beautiful objects,' she declared. 'I had not appreciated until this moment how old some of the furniture is at Pitlochry House. I must look at it properly when we get back.'

'Yes, my great-aunt and great-uncle bought some good pieces of antique Cape furniture and silver. Cape Town is full of eighteenth and early nineteenth century silver, glass, porcelain, furniture and paintings. Have you heard of Groot Constantia?'

'Oh yes, I remember reading about it – an old manor house and wine estate, isn't it?'

'That's right,' Richard agreed. 'We must visit it someday. It's full of things like these, and its setting is particularly lovely.'

The exhibits in the Castle Military Museum were of rather less interest to Antonia, although Richard seemed quite enthused by the collection of antique weapons. This evidence of the boy still present in Richard, Antonia found quite touching. There was a collection of flintlock and percussion cap pistols and muskets on display, and Richard spent some time eagerly explaining to Antonia the difference between their mechanisms, and why the percussion cap was an advance over the flintlock. Antonia (although she could not be said to have shared in Richard's keen interest) smiled at his enthusiasm, and slipped her arm through his, and the gesture struck Richard as so natural, that he gave it no further thought.

They entered the house via the back door, having first garaged the car. Katy, who was waiting for them, gave a bark of greeting. Richard bent and caressed the dog's head and ears.

'Who's a good girl?' he addressed Katy. 'Who's glad to see her Dad?' The dog's tail wagged frantically and Antonia smiled. They walked past the kitchen and the domestic offices.

'Thank you for a super day, Richard,' said Antonia. 'And thank you for the lovely boots.' She did not immediately free the hand that Richard had seized hold of once he had finished petting Katy.

'I enjoyed myself too,' he told her. And he had: he had experienced the day as a singularly happy one. Had Helen ever made him feel so content? Perhaps during the first few years of their marriage – but if so, he could not remember the occasions now. He did not think that he had ever felt so perfectly at ease in Helen's company as he had felt today in that of his young English cousin. By the time they had reached the hallway and the front of the building, Richard had let go of Antonia's hand.

'Would you join me in a drink on the veranda?' he asked her.

'Yes, I'd like that, Richard.'

André had been about to set up at the bar counter. Richard greeted him and asked him to take Katy into the garden for ten minutes. The couple then greeted the scattering of guests still sitting on the veranda after tea. As they sat down, Miss Chelmsford-Spruce regarded them with a knowing but tolerant eye. They had been the subject of gossip among the old ladies in the hotel for some time. One or two of these thought that Richard must be having an affair with the young English girl, and that this was the reason his wife had left him, but Miss Chelmsford-Spruce, who greeted the couple cheerily, was partisan for Richard. 'Nonsense!' she told Mrs. Hapgood, her crony, who was sitting with her on the veranda. (She moderated the volume of her usually somewhat carrying voice as she spoke). 'I foresaw Mrs. Channing's eventual departure long before Miss Bingham had even arrived.'

'Well, perhaps so,' Mrs. Hapgood conceded. 'But I do think it's scandalous, the way they're together all the time.'

'Oh, Millicent!' Miss Chelmsford-Spruce declared in exasperation. 'Why should they not spend time together? Miss Bingham is Mr. Channing's cousin, after all – and it was Mrs. Channing who abandoned him, sneaking away like that, not the other way around.'

And so the two old ladies had to agree to disagree, for they were old friends by now.

Richard and Antonia sat in contented silence with their drinks. Richard had a large Irish whiskey on the table in front of him. It took a good deal more than just one large whiskey for Richard to become noticeably loquacious, Antonia had soon realised. She was drinking a Hanepoort desert wine, made from grapes that were grown and processed not so very far away. The sweet, fruity bouquet appealed to her somewhat uneducated girl's palate. How wonderful, she sometimes thought, to be staying in a wine producing country! Indeed, as the summer set in, the landscape and the climate had begun to remind her of a holiday she had once spent with her family on Italy's Amalfi Coast.

They sat there with Katy (whom André had returned a while ago) lying at their feet, until the blood orange orb of the setting sun appeared from beneath a bank of low cloud far across the sea in the west, and the cloud turned the colour of coral and tangerine on its undersides. Every evening now, the setting sun had moved a little further towards the south. In the narrow band between the horizon and the cloudbank above, the sky took on tones of crimson and scarlet as the fiery ball struck the rim of the sea. Within a few minutes, the sun was gone, and although for a while the clouds were glowing vermilion, deepening to maroon, the sky above them darkened by gradual degrees. The evening star appeared above the cloudbank, and the air felt suddenly chill.

'Let's go inside, Richard,' said Antonia, breaking their silence. 'It's growing cold.'

'Yes, it is growing chilly,' Richard agreed. They stood and went inside. It was still just about cold enough at night for a fire to be appreciated, and Charlie the man-of-all-work had lighted a fire in one of the two big fireplaces in the great hall, before ending his duties for the day. Most of the damage done by the firebombs to the windows, to the floor below them, and to the woodwork either side of them, had been repaired, but the badly scorched and burned folding interior shutters, which had had to be removed, had not been replaced. Richard had not yet found anyone who could or would make new folding shutters. Although Richard often begrudged the expense of upkeep on other parts of the house, he knew that the great hall was the heart of the house, and the damage must be attended to. New velvet curtains had been hung too, but Richard had cursed the insurers, who, as he had feared, had refused to cover the cost of the repairs.

Antonia finished her glass of wine. 'That was nice. Thanks. I must go upstairs to change,' she told Richard with a smile, as she stood up. She was looking forward to dinner: it had been a long and active day. Richard too stood, then, as the young woman left, he sat down again, lighting another cigarette. He did not need to change for dinner: he was already wearing a tie and jacket.

The residents at Pitlochry House Hotel had grown inured to the images of violence and unrest – most such incidents taking place in and around Johannesburg, but with occasional outbreaks elsewhere in the country, including the Cape Coloured districts of the Cape Flats – that periodically appeared on the television news in the evening. Images that would once have been shocking and distressing in the extreme, no longer had the same impact on the viewer. But the anger felt by the black and Coloured communities burned as bright as ever, and the marches, labour strikes, occasional riots, and destructive outbreaks of violence in the black and Coloured townships, continued through to the end of that year, and beyond. In Cape Town, however, the city centre did not again have to witness the police resorting to gunfire and teargas; indeed, for most Europeans in South Africa, the unrest was something that happened in black and Coloured districts, and did not much affect them.

Nor did anyone at Pitlochry House (or, indeed, many whites in South Africa) pay much attention to the periodic reports in the newspapers of ecclesiastical anti-Apartheid activism. Churchmen such as the Rt. Rev. Bill Burnett (who would prove to be the last white Anglican Archbishop of Cape Town, and the last white Metropolitan of the Anglican Church in South Africa), the Rev. Trevor Huddleston (another Anglican cleric), the Rev. Beyers Naudé (a rare anti-Apartheid voice within the Dutch Reformed Church), the Roman Catholic Archbishop Denis Hurley, and the black Anglican Bishop Desmond Tutu, were all prominent in the clerical anti-Apartheid movement. If anything, such activity on the part of the Church tended to alienate many whites, the majority of whom accepted the institution of Apartheid, and the inevitability of white rule, unquestioningly, for it seemed to them self evident (looking at the sorry condition of the independent blacks states to the north) that the blacks were unable by and large to manage their own affairs.

Yet the last few months of racial tension and extreme unrest were leaving their mark on the European community no less than they had altered the way many among the Cape Coloured and black communities now regarded themselves. For many among South Africa's whites, the perception that they were now a beleaguered minority had gained in force, and the more astute were beginning for the first time to consider emigration sometime in the future. (During the next several decades, Britain, Australia-New Zealand, America and Ireland, would become destinations of choice for a growing number of white South Africans). The residents at Pitlochry House Hotel, however, were too old to consider such a move, even had they wished to, and Richard identified too intimately with both Pitlochry House and the Cape Peninsula, a region he had grown to love, to wish to return to an England which he knew (from what he read and heard) had changed enormously since his departure in 1956.

Towards the end of October, Helen's parents contacted Richard, suggesting that their daughter might be open to a reconciliation with her husband.

'Helen's parents write of a possible "reconciliation" between Helen and myself,' Richard told Antonia. 'I wouldn't say no, if there was a chance it meant Jeremy coming home.' The two were out hiking in the mountains. It was the last

Saturday in October, almost the end of the month. They had left Pitlochry House immediately after breakfast, and had begun their day's hike at the highest point of Constantia Nek, leaving the car in the clearing beneath the Scots pines which grew across the road from the restaurant, and had then followed the narrow, un-metalled vehicular trail known as the Jeep Track, as it wound its way along the side of the mountain, making a fairly gentle ascent to the Back Table. It was an attractive and a popular walk, the trail making its way at first through dark, still, pine forest, but in due course the forest was left spread out below them as they climbed higher, affording them a magnificent view which took in much of the Cape Flats and the distant mountain ranges beyond, as well as the northern sweep of False Bay, with the jagged peaks of the Hottentots Holland range visible beyond its further shores.

Antonia was wearing her new hiking boots in earnest for the first time (although she had already worn them a few times, for occasional strolls of no great distance with Richard and Katy, not very far from Pitlochry House). She was pleased with them. She was wearing rather short navy blue shorts, and a fairly tight, plain white tee-shirt, with a floppy white cotton hat on her short honey-blonde hair. She carried a pullover in the small knapsack on her back. Richard had not realised until now that he had not seen her wearing shorts before. He found it difficult not to stare at her long legs each time they halted to admire the view. They were so shapely, so supple and strong and youthful, he thought – and so pale! Such creamy, white, unblemished skin was rarely seen in the Cape Peninsula in Richard's experience; skin that had been, until now, untouched by the sun.

The day was warming rapidly, and the sun was already hot. About halfway through the ascent they paused in their hike, and Richard, who wore no hat, mopped his face with a large handkerchief. "I don't get enough exercise anymore," he thought. Tiny, jewel-like Sunbirds – their colours bright and iridescent – flitted from flower to flower on the steep slope. Somewhere not very far away, Antonia could hear the bark of a baboon.

'Agh!' Richard exclaimed. 'Let's forget about Helen. It's far too lovely up here to bother with her right now.'

There was a seepage from a rock face to their left, and a shallow pool of clear water no more than a few feet across had formed at the edge of the road. Richard knelt and scooped some water into his mouth, then he splashed his face. He called Antonia across.

'See here, Antonia – there – those small plants. They're called sundews, and they're carnivorous. If you look closely, you can see tiny insects, which the sundews are busy digesting, trapped inside their leaves. Do you see?'

'Oh – yes – I see them,' responded Antonia, bending down alongside Richard. 'I would never have guessed.'

'Right-O,' said Richard, getting to his feet. 'It's not very far to the top now. Let's carry on.' And they began walking again.

They reached the comparatively level plateau of the Back Table soon after eleven o' clock. They were now well over two thousand feet above sea level. To their right was the water overseer's cottage, a sturdy structure of cut and dressed stone. Richard had always thought how wonderful it must be to live way up here. On their left was the De Villiers Dam, the smallest of the five dams on top of Table Mountain, and below the high dam wall lay Orange Kloof, deep, steep sided and heavily wooded with indigenous tree cover. Antonia was entranced by the rugged beauty of the scene. After a while she shrugged her little backpack free, and reached out the water canteen within it, and took a long drink. Richard extracted a leather bound, silver hip flask from his pocket, engraved with his initials (it had belonged to his grandfather, whose initials Richard shared), gulped from it (in the flask was neat Irish whiskey, and it was his first drink of the day), then took a more conventional drink from his own water bottle.

Antonia turned to Richard. 'Thank you for bringing me up here, Richard,' she said, her eyes shining.

Impulsively, Richard took two steps towards her and took her face between his hands, and bent his head and kissed her on the mouth. To his immense gratification, the kiss was enthusiastically returned. They stood together, the kiss prolonged for what seemed a period outside of measurable time, then Antonia managed to disengage her lips from Richard's and break free from his grasp, saying, her voice rather breathless, 'I don't think we should …'

'I'm in love with you, Antonia,' declared Richard earnestly. 'You do know that, don't you?'

'Yes, I think I knew that, Richard. But where can it go, if Helen's going to be coming back?'

'Ohhh …' Richard sighed. 'I know.' He smiled suddenly,

a somewhat wistful smile. 'Let's push on,' he said, his voice not entirely even. 'We have a way to go if we're to reach the top cable station restaurant in time for lunch.'

Chapter Fourteen

The trail – of rocky quartzite and eroded sandstone – took the two of them via fairly level ground past the long, narrow Alexandra Dam, then past the equally long and narrow Victoria Dam, both of which lay to their right. The dams' further shores backed against pine forest,[*] and the contrast between the shadowed gloom of the trees across the water, and the sun-baked and glaring terrain through which they walked, was marked. Antonia was fascinated by this mountain top environment, a world she had little expected to find.

'I had no idea the top of Table Mountain looked like this!' she declared. 'We could be miles from anywhere!'

Richard, who had been silent since they had recommenced their hike (perhaps regretting his ill-considered and emotional outburst a little while earlier), gave a short laugh. 'We're nowhere near the top, yet, Antonia,' he told her. 'This

---

[*] The pine forests atop Table Mountain were felled by over-zealous ecological purists in the 1980s. With this act of vandalism, much of the sense of mystery and wonder experienced by the hiker on top of Table Mountain has gone for good.

is the Back Table, a good deal lower than the Front Table, or Table Mountain proper – as you will see.'

They left the sunshine behind as they entered the cool, dark pine forest. The narrow trail, strewn with pine needles and pine cones, was hemmed in by trees either side. The resin scented gloom enveloped them, and the silence was profound. Antonia was unprepared for the next scene, for without any warning (at least, Antonia had no warning), they found themselves leaving the forest, and immediately in front of them lay another dam, this one broad and long, the impact of its still, dark waters, a deep shade of tannin, only partially relieved by the sunshine glinting on the water's surface.

'My gosh!' Antonia exclaimed. There was, she thought, something rather sinister about the dark water.

'This is the Hely-Hutchinson Dam,' Richard told her.

'How old are these dams?' asked Antonia.

'Late nineteenth century,' Richard replied. 'They were built – obviously – to supply Cape Town with water.'

They reached the far side of the dam via the walkway along the top of the dam wall itself, which was built of enormous cut and dressed blocks of granite. To their left as they crossed over, some distance below them, lay another broad body of dark water, which Richard told Antonia was the Woodhead Dam. On the far side of the crossing, their path swung sharply to the right. Now, only for the first time since they had set out on their hike, they came across another group – a trio of hikers drawing near. As they passed, the two groups wished each other a good day, and continued on their way.

'We will be climbing to the Front Table soon,' Richard, who was in the lead, announced. And indeed, after a short while the path swung to the north again, and began a fairly gradual ascent, climbing more steeply as the narrow trail passed between large outcrops of rock. In one of these broken stretches, Richard came to a sudden halt.

'Antonia, come up to me slowly,' he said.

Wondering, Antonia did so, and when she was almost level with Richard, he pointed at the sun-lit dusty ground about five feet before him. 'Do you see it?' he asked. 'A puff adder.'

'Oh!' exclaimed Antonia, looking with fascinated horror at the grey-brown, rather fat serpent with a pale zigzag pattern on its back. 'Are they poisonous?'

'Extremely. And they're a lazy snake – often, they wont move out of your way until the last moment, by which time, you've been bitten.'

They stared at the creature, which lay immobile, then Richard asked Antonia to step backwards a few paces. She did so, and he bent and picked up a small pebble, which he chucked underarm just before the snake. The puff adder opened its jaws angrily and hissed – Antonia had never heard a snake hiss before – then slowly moved off the path, describing a series of "S's".

'Now you know why we wear boots when we're hiking in the Cape,' Richard remarked. They passed the spot where the puff adder had retreated into the low scrub growth, Antonia rather glad to leave the creature behind them. But for a while thereafter she kept darting glances on the ground ahead of her.

They were still talking about snakes in Africa – Richard had a rich fund of stories, some of them rather horrific – when at last the trail levelled out, and suddenly, there was revealed an extraordinary view across the Cape Flats, far, far below. Antonia realised that they were much higher now. She halted, and stood staring at the panoramic scene.

'Those mountains in the distance,' she remarked, 'How mysterious they seem.'

'For many years,' Richard responded, 'they defined the limits of the Cape Colony. It was a long time before anyone other than elephant hunters made their way through and beyond them.'

It was by now very warm, with the sun at its zenith. They had left the sheltering forest behind once they crossed the Hely-Hutchinson Dam. Each took another drink of water from their water canteens, and Richard, no longer as fit as he had been in years past, mopped his face with his handkerchief once again. Antonia, however, merely glowed – thought Richard. "What a wonderful, down-to-earth sort of a girl!" he thought. So refreshing, after his wife's often overblown, extreme femininity. Richard had never succeeded in getting Helen to join him in a hike in the mountains.

Continuing on their way, Richard once again naturally taking the lead (and any snakes around will meet Richard first, thought Antonia!), the pair followed the trail as it made its final ascent, following a winding course between large outcrops of naked rock, and at last they reached the highest point on the Front Table, a white painted trigonometrical beacon (these were popularly referred to as "trig beacons") known as Maclear's Beacon, surrounded by a spreading heap of rocks and stones (placed there by people heeding some atavistic urging to acknowledge this, the highest point on Table Mountain).

If the view before had impressed and amazed Antonia, this panorama now left her speechless. Her gaze took in a wide sweep of ocean, bounded by the west coast shore as it marched northwards into the distance, with the great bulk of Devil's Peak (whose crest was not very much lower than the point where they stood) almost directly in front of them, separated from Table Mountain by a deep saddle. Away to the noth-east, Antonia could see the far mountain ranges she had earlier remarked on. To her left, the level Table Top extended towards the west. When she turned around, she could see the entire mountainous length of the Cape Peninsula, extending far to the south, and to the south-south-east, False Bay, its waters a deep shining blue, was now visible in its entirety. The clarity of the light and the sense of extreme elevation, of an almost god-like perspective of the World, felt intoxicating.

When at last speech returned to her, Antonia declared, 'I have never seen such an amazing view in all my life.'

Richard grinned with pleasure. 'I felt like you, the first time I came up here, in 1956. We're over three thousand, five hundred feet above sea level now. I've known it snow up here during winter. Right-O, how do you feel about some lunch?'

They followed the path along the length of the top of Table Mountain. At one point the trail approached the edge of the Table, and the view of the City Bowl, far, far below, left Antonia silent again. She saw the city, with its harbour, laid out like some architect's model; the tiny ships in the harbour were like toys. Then she noticed what appeared to be an island, far out in Table Bay, and she spoke again.

'That island – what is it, Richard?'

'That's our very own Devil's Island,' Richard replied. 'It's Robben Island, a prison island, where maximum security and political prisoners are incarcerated.'

'Who was Robin?' asked Antonia.

'"*Robben*,"' Richard said, giving the word an Afrikaans pronunciation, and spelling it for Antonia. 'It's the plural of "seal" in Dutch: "Seal Island."'

At the western end of the Table was the top cable station, where the cable car docked. Not far from this tall, weathered concrete structure was a pretty building of dressed stone, with a steeply pitched roof, crow-stepped gables at either end, a chimney at one end, and a bay window at each of the two nearer corners. Richard had always thought that this was one of the most charming, architecturally perfect buildings he had ever seen; an oasis of comfort and refreshment for hikers and cable car visitors alike. He had of course lunched here several times before, the first time in company with his friend Michael, with whom he had driven the length of Africa in 1956.

'Oh, Richard! A proper restaurant!' exclaimed Antonia, when Richard told her they would be lunching there. 'I'm not dressed for a restaurant.'

'You look lovely,' Richard assured her (and he thought she looked adorable, her complexion made rosy by the sun; her innocent girl's long legs), 'and they're used to casually dressed hikers in the restaurant.'

For lunch they both ate yellowtail, pan fried in butter. Antonia found she had an enormous appetite, and she scoffed two bread rolls, well buttered, while waiting for the fish to arrive. She drank two glasses of cool Cape white wine during the meal; Richard drank two Castle lagers, downing the first lager at a tremendous rate. He ordered Cape brandy pudding for himself for dessert, but Antonia (once Richard had explained that it consisted of a sweet pastry crust containing a custard filling) chose *melktert*.

Antonia felt that the conversation during the meal was a trifle constrained. This was, she thought, probably her own fault. Essentially (quite aside from the difference in their ages), she and Richard had very little in common. Richard's recollection of life in England was two decades out of date; the swinging sixties had passed him by – why, he still spoke of ducktails and teddy boys! And unlike Antonia, who had spent one summer vacation after another in France, Richard had visited France no more than once or twice. Usually, these differences did not matter very much, for she generally felt very comfortable in Richard's company, but his heartfelt declaration of love for her earlier that day, while not at all shocking, had begun, on reflection, to feel a little disconcerting. Antonia certainly felt enormously attracted to Richard, and perhaps she was at least half in love with him – but to move their relationship on from its present comfortable condition would, she thought, lead only to unhappiness. Perhaps, had there not been the possibility of Helen's returning to Pitlochry House, she might have chanced a love affair. As it was, she felt very cautious – but she hoped for now that Richard would make no further declarations of that nature, and that their relationship could resume its easy course.

As for poor Richard, he had long been experiencing both anguish and joy at the same time in Antonia's company; he hardly knew how he was going to endure. "I must try not to make a fool of myself," he thought. And he really hoped that Helen would not be coming back – but again, there was Jeremy to consider: if it was the only way of getting Jeremy back, he would have to try to make a go of it. But, oh God! How he yearned to possess Antonia!

And so each of them was rather silent during that meal high above Cape Town, and each hoped that with the passage of time, their situation would become clearer – and easier.

And indeed, by the time they reached the Land Rover again, parked across the road from the restaurant, at the highest point of the *Nek*, they were feeling easier with each other once again, having walked off their slight mutual awkwardness. Both were feeling somewhat weary, but it was an honest weariness, which left them feeling content, and Richard was looking forward to sitting on the veranda with a drink – or several – before dinner. However, he felt obliged to offer Antonia some tea before they set off for Pitlochry House.

'Would you like some tea and scones, Antonia?' he asked. 'The restaurant across the road serves a good afternoon tea.'

Antonia thought a moment, then replied, 'I think I would rather get on home, Richard; I'm feeling quite worn out.'

'Yes, you're right. We'll head straight home then.'

It was half past six before they reached Pitlochry House

(was it, wondered Richard, at all significant that Antonia now referred to it as "home"?), and both of them went upstairs to have a wash, and change out of their hiking gear. They met downstairs again at about a quarter past seven. Both had had time for a quick shower. (Antonia's was one of the few guest bedrooms with an *en suite* bathroom, lavatory and shower).

Before an appreciative scattering of Saturday evening visitors standing and sitting at the veranda (come from as far away as Cape Town, to have a drink or two, and perhaps a meal, and watch the sun going down), the sun – a huge great ball of ruddy-orange – was just dipping below the horizon, and the narrow horizontal bands of cloud in the western sky were aflame with colour: burnt orange on their undersides, and apricot and lemon yellow on top. Antonia was thinking, as she so frequently did, that she had never lived anywhere with such a sublime view, nor anywhere with as magnificent a setting. She smiled at Richard as he approached her with the Cinzano *Rosso* with lemonade she had asked for. He had decided against a whiskey, but had requested a cold lager from André, serving behind the bar counter, for he felt a touch dehydrated after their day in the mountains. Richard handed the Cinzano to Antonia, and sat down across the little table from her. Katy, who was delighted to have her master back home after a long day's absence, flopped onto the polished concrete floor alongside his chair. 'Cheers!' Richard said, raising his glass of lager.

'Cheers,' Antonia responded, raising her long narrow glass, the ice clinking in it, in return.

The number of long stay residents (which, to Richard's gratification, had recently risen to nine) was exceeded several times over on Friday and Saturday nights by the number of casual visitors; groups of two, three, or four people, come for an early evening drink. During the winter months there would be live music on offer, but during the summer, although there was no live music, meals were served – and of course, in summertime there were the splendid sunsets across the sea, an enormous draw: during the winter period, the sun went down behind the mountain; you could not in wintertime see the sunset from Pitlochry House Hotel. However, once the summer set in, there were remarkable sunsets on display again, as the sun set further and further towards the south, far across the ocean. These displays were famed across the region. There were few easily accessible locations on the Peninsula with such commanding views of the sunset, and people came from as far afield as Cape Town proper to admire them. The visitors on summer evenings were generally a little older, and more smartly dressed, than the crowd the hotel often saw on a Friday or Saturday night during the winter, come to enjoy the live music.

During the summer months, Elsbet the Cook, and her assistants in the kitchen, were on duty later than usual on Friday and Saturday nights, and meals were served until nine o'clock. These were traditional dishes, easily prepared: steak and chips was always popular (how the South Africans loved their steak, thought Antonia), as was fish and chips. The two hotel maids, Bella and Marta, were very busy serving as waitresses on Friday and Saturday evenings, and André too was busy behind his bar counter in the great hall.

Antonia, who felt that Friday and Saturday evenings at the hotel were something of an occasion, and who was excited by the atmosphere generated by a large number of visitors having a good time, had changed into a rather elegant cocktail dress of finely woven, deep green wool after her shower. She wore an engraved gold pendant on a gold chain around her neck. She had found time to apply some makeup to her face. Richard thought she looked stunning.

'You look lovely,' he told her, when she came back downstairs.

'Thank you,' Antonia replied with a smile, gratified at Richard's compliment. 'And you are looking rather smart, too, Richard.' He was wearing fawn slacks, in which the creases were still apparent, and a navy blue blazer, with a rather striking tie, which was distinguished by broad, diagonal maroon and black stripes.

'Is that your old school tie, or your college tie?' Antonia asked him, having taken a sip from her drink.

Richard, who was feeling in an unusually good mood (he had quite forgotten his anxiety earlier that day in Antonia's company), grinned. 'College,' he replied. 'Exeter College. It's rather startling, isn't it?'

Antonia's laughter was light and happy. 'I think it's super,' she said. 'What did you read at university?'

'As little as I could get away with!' Richard laughed heartily. 'No – I took Modern History and English. Do you have any plans yourself for college?'

'I was thinking of reading Classics – Latin and Greek. But of course it will have to be next October, now.'

'My gosh, you must be a lot brighter than I am!' Richard

exclaimed. 'I couldn't make much sense of Latin, and as for Greek – well, it would be all Greek to me!' He laughed again. He was in fine spirits. Antonia laughed in return, amused by Richard's obvious pleasure in his pun. She was glad to see him so happy and light hearted: it seemed that his amorous declaration on the mountain was not, after all, going to get in the way of their friendship.

Richard had time to follow his two Castle lagers (gosh, how fast they went down!) with a large Irish whiskey – gulp-gulp – before the two of them went inside for dinner. Despite a momentary recollection of his earlier awkwardness in Antonia's company, he was feeling rather cheerful. The day's exercise had agreed with him.

Chapter Fifteen

By mid November there had been no move as yet towards a formal reconciliation between Helen and Richard. Helen's parents (Richard had always got on fairly well with her father in the past) remained, however, in periodic communication with him, and so he was not entirely cut off from news of his son. Jeremy was studying hard for his forthcoming Matric examinations, the outcome of which would determine whether or not he gained the place he sought at the University of Cape Town. Nobody entertained any real doubts on that score, but it was nonetheless a stressful period for the boy.

Did it trouble Jeremy that his mother and father were separated? It had been quite a few years since he had last held his father in very much esteem, and perhaps his parents' separation meant little to him. Especially as both his mother and his grandparents indulged and spoiled him. His grandfather had already promised him a car when he turned eighteen in April next year. Yet Jeremy had a secret ambition of which not even his mother was aware: that before too many years had passed, his father might have handed the strategic management of Pitlochry House Hotel over to him, and with his grandparents' wealth behind him, he could turn it into the sort of five star, luxury destination for foreign visitors that his father had only ever dreamed of doing. And in so doing, he would have shown his father that he, Jeremy, was the better man of the two.

But should his parents divorce one another, his chances of gaining control of Pitlochry House Hotel one day might, he feared, be much diminished. This was what Jeremy, who was not often afraid (why should he be? Everything had always come easily to him; there had been little occasion in his life for doubts or fears), was now afraid of.

Thus it was that even while Jeremy felt little respect for his father, and had no emotional investment in his parents staying together, he yet wished them to remain together, so as not to place in jeopardy his chances of gaining control of the hotel one day.

In fact, it was not very easy to obtain a divorce in South Africa at that time: a divorce could be granted only in cases of adultery, malicious desertion, insanity, and habitual criminal behaviour. The irretrievable breakdown of a marriage would only be recognised from 1979 onwards as a reason for granting a divorce.

At Pitlochry House, Richard did not miss his wife, whom he would be happy never to see again. But he missed his son, to whom he felt an obligation. Although he longed to be free in every sense to pay his suit to Antonia, he baulked at actually taking the initiative in obtaining a divorce from Helen. Instead, he rather hoped that Helen would drop any ideas of a reconciliation, and request that he provide her with grounds for her obtaining a divorce. He was sure that he could convince any private investigator she might hire that he was having an adulterous affair with his young cousin. But that would be wrong, and if Helen gained a divorce on such grounds, he supposed that he would have to pay alimony to her. And really, he could not afford to do that.

And so, Richard suffered agonies of doubt, uncertainty and indecision; not sure what he wanted, not sure what course would be best; sure only that he desired Antonia with every fibre of his being – but that he could offer her nothing more right now than an adulterous affair. And not only would that be hugely unfair to her (Richard was in fact a good chap, with a strong sense of morality), he doubted anyway that Antonia would be willing to accept such an arrangement.

The days were very warm now. The sky (excepting only for the iconic summer "tablecloth" of flat white cloud above Table Mountain itself) was nearly always cloudless, a blue so intense it seemed almost to vibrate with depth and purity. More often than not, there was a wind blowing, the South-Easter, known to some as the "Cape Doctor," on the grounds that it rid Cape Town of disease and pollution. At Pitlochry House they did not experience the wind as strongly on their side of the mountain, but it could often be felt along the False Bay coast.

One Saturday morning towards the end of November, Richard said to Antonia over breakfast, 'Would you like to come sailing today? It's been too long since I took the yacht out.'

'I would love that,' Antonia replied. 'What should I wear?'

'Shorts will do, and tennis shoes, and a hat – and bring a pullover or a cardigan. It can get quite cold on the water, even though the sun is shining.'

Richard telephoned his friend, John, who lived in Simon's Town, and asked him how strong the wind was over there. John had sailed with Richard occasionally; he understood how to talk about the wind strength in sailing terms.

'I'd say it's blowing a moderate breeze, Rick. Of course, it'll be stronger out in the Bay. You thinking of going sailing, are you?'

'Yeah ... Antonia has never gone sailing, so she's told me – if you discount dinghy sailing on inland waters. And I've not taken *Felicitations* out since May this year.'

John had met Antonia, his friend's very attractive young cousin of some degree, when Richard had taken her for lunch at the Lord Collingwood. John had guessed almost immediately that there was more to Richard's interest in the girl than mere familial regard. However, John knew that while his friend might flirt with pretty young women occasionally, he was no philanderer, and so he could not guess at the depth of his friend's feelings for the young woman.

Richard and Antonia left Pitlochry House at about nine-thirty, and they had reached Simon's Town by a quarter past ten. The False Bay Yacht Club is located on Simon's Town's harbour front. There is a lawn in front of the club house with several wooden tables with benches either side, where members and their guests can sit in the sun and enjoy a drink and something to eat. There is a slipway, where boats can be winched out of the water, and a hard, where work can be done on them. *Felicitations* was a Hunter Europa, a development of a nineteen foot daysailer. It had a fin keel, a beam of six feet, and a displacement of one and a half thousand pounds. There were two bunks below (along with a small portable chemical toilet that Richard had obtained, although this was not often resorted to), and a fair amount of stowage space. For the rare occasions that Richard might wish to cook on board, he had a small gas camping stove which would be set up in the cockpit.

'What a pretty boat,' Antonia remarked. And she was. The little yacht was well proportioned and graceful to look at. She was winched onto the hard on a dolly, and her hull scraped down and repainted by the club's boat maintenance crew, every September, and Richard paid a young chap, who had occasionally served as "crew" for him, to scrub the deposits from the sea birds from the deck once a week – so the little boat presented a trim appearance to Antonia's eye. (*Felicitations* was small enough not to require "crew," but as Jeremy no longer sailed with his father, Richard enjoyed this young man's company occasionally in his stead).

'It's so cosy below!' Antonia exclaimed, looking into the saloon. 'And is that ... yes ... there's even a loo!'

'Yes, there is. I've overnighted in her two or three times,' Richard remarked.

It was about a quarter past eleven before they were ready to cast off. Antonia found the preparations interesting, in particular, rigging the sails.

They sailed up the east coast of the Peninsula on a broad reach, between a quarter and half a mile offshore, but drawing quite near to the shore in Fish Hoek Bay (near enough to see that the beach was crowded with bathers), then continuing the short distance to Kalk Bay. Whitecaps crested the surface of the sea, and periodically, cold spray flew back from the bows and slapped them in the face. The first time this happened, Antonia gave a little shriek, but on subsequent occasions she merely laughed. Both of them wore floppy cotton hats. Antonia, following Richard's advice, had applied sun cream to her bare limbs. (Richard had tried not to stare so hard as she had rubbed the lotion into her long legs. Was "marbled" the word, he had wondered? No – that put him in mind of a side of beef in a butcher's shop; "velvety" or perhaps "satiny" were better choices). She had also applied the sun cream to her pretty nose and the tops of her cheeks. ('There's a powerful glare from the water,' Richard had warned her). She wore a fairly tight tee-shirt with rather brief shorts, with a pullover knotted loosely over her shoulders, and Richard was wearing baggy khaki shorts (the same shorts he had gone hiking in), and a sleeveless padded top over his tee-shirt. Unlike Antonia, who was so obviously English, Richard had a warm brown tan. With occasional spray slapping at them, their clothes were damp at times, but the sun burned bright and hot, and their clothes did not remain damp for long between soakings.

Offshore from the commercial fishing harbour of Kalk Bay, they set a new course, this time on a close reach as far as Seal Island, which lay a long way out in the Bay, directly due east from Kalk Bay. On their way, despite the small yacht's lively motion, they ate some of the cheese and pickles sandwiches that Elsbet had prepared for them.

'You're a good sailor,' Richard remarked, as the small boat both pitched and rolled. The wind and waves were more pronounced this far out in the huge Bay.

'I'm rather relieved – I wasn't sure I wouldn't be feeling seasick,' Antonia responded.

They followed their sandwiches with sweetened black coffee from a Thermos flask. Richard added a large tot of Irish whiskey to his coffee, from the silver hip flask he carried in one of the pockets of his padded jacket. He smoked one of the few cigarettes he was to light up during their sail. Antonia could now see an extensive, shallow outcrop of rock arising from the sea some distance ahead. Having circled the sprawling island of dark, bare rock – Antonia exclaiming with pleasure at the sharp snouted seals sporting in the water – they commenced a long, broad reach back to Simon's Town, making their mooring around tea time.

Neither had spoken much during the sail, but the long periods of silence had not been awkward ones. Each had been lost in the moment, in the boat's motion, in the movement of the sea. Richard had forgotten that time ceased to have any meaning while sailing a small boat; that there was no sense of its passing. His mind had been empty of troubled thoughts; there was very little active consciousness at work; his handling of the boat, a living thing, needful of the empathetic bond he felt for her, was carried out quite unconsciously.

Richard had encouraged Antonia to drink frequently from the large bottle of water they had with them, or from the bottle of orange squash that Elsbet had mixed. He himself drank often from the water bottle. He knew from experience, that with the combination of burning sun, wind, and ocean glare, it was easy to become dehydrated out on the water. He barely touched his silver hip flask. But despite their efforts to remain hydrated, both of them felt somewhat burned out, but deeply content, by the time they reached the mooring jetty. It took them a while to strip the sails from the rigging, fold and stow them below, and remove the small outboard motor from the transom and stow it below also. It was closer to five o' clock when they finally made their way to the club house, where Richard greeted a couple of people he knew. The club house was busy, this Saturday afternoon.

'Haven't seen you around for a while, Rick,' one of these acquaintances remarked, shaking Richard's hand. 'How are you keeping?'

'I'm fine thanks, Tim. Just trying to stay one step ahead every day – you know how it is.'

The man laughed. 'Yeah – I know how it is.' He was staring at Antonia's long legs, which had a rosy blush from the sun.

'Tim, this is Antonia, a cousin of mine visiting from England for a while.'

'How do you do, Antonia?' Tim shook her hand.

They found a small table on the club house deck, looking out over the harbour. Across the harbour they could see the lean grey forms of a South African Navy corvette and a destroyer, moored against a far quayside. Richard asked Antonia what she would like to drink. 'And I'll get us some toasted sandwiches too. Would you like that?'

'That sounds a good idea, Richard,' Antonia replied. 'I'll have a Cinzano with lemonade, please.' Antonia (who was now wearing her pullover) thanked Richard for the long, tall Cinzano *Rosso* and lemonade that he brought her, while Richard himself hugely appreciated the first of the two ice cold lagers he was to down in rapid succession. And each ate a couple of the toasted cheese and tomato sandwiches, to address the growling emptiness in their middles.

'I must go sailing more often,' Richard remarked. 'I had forgotten how much I enjoy it.'

'I enjoyed myself too,' Antonia responded. 'And when I took the tiller, I could feel the boat, like … like a living creature. Sailing a dinghy doesn't begin to compare.'

'Oh yes! They are like living creatures. That's why we ascribe personalities to sailing boats, and why we call them "she."'

'"She?"' remarked Antonia. 'But why "she," not "he"?'

Richard grinned and put his glass of beer down. 'Because boats, like a woman, need gentling and understanding if you're to get the best out of them.'

'Oh, you … you man!' exclaimed Antonia. But she laughed.

It was about half past six by the time they garaged the Land Rover in the old stables behind Pitlochry House. Despite the toasted cheese and tomato sandwiches they had consumed at the club house (Antonia had ate two, Richard four), each of them was looking forward to dinner. Antonia went upstairs. ("I'll have to wash my hair, too," she thought. "It's full of salt.") She would be changing into something more suitable for a Saturday evening. (There were already some visitors present, eager to watch the sunset, drinks in hand). Richard, with a happy Katy at his side, checked with

Mrs. Stoddart for any issues or news he should be made aware of. Mrs. Stoddart did not normally work Saturday afternoons, but she had come in in response to a telephone call from Richard before he and Antonia had set off that morning.

'No walk-ins?' Richard asked her. 'No new bookings?'

'I'm afraid not, Mr. Channing,' the good woman answered. 'But there is something that's been troubling me. It's Mrs. Hapgood.'

'What about the old dear?' Richard asked.

'I've noticed that she really struggles with the stairs now,' Mrs. Stoddart replied. 'Cant we move her down a floor, to a room on the first floor?'

'That would mean one less first floor room available for guests prepared to pay for it,' Richard responded. 'I doubt Mrs. Hapgood can afford an increase in her rate.'

'I was thinking we would keep the same rate, Mr. Channing.'

Richard was in a good mood after his day on the ocean. 'Oh, alright,' he conceded. 'Have you a room in mind?'

'Yes, I was thinking, one of the mountain view rooms at the back. Mrs. Hapgood wouldn't mind the lack of a sea view, if it meant she had one flight less to climb to reach her room.'

'You haven't talked to her about it already, have you?'

Mrs. Stoddart looked offended. 'Of course not, Mr. Channing!'

'We'll do it, then,' Richard said. 'And you're a kind soul, Mrs. Stoddart. I'll talk to her at dinner.'

After Richard had taken Katy for a short outing, returning as it was growing fully dark (what a splendid sunset it had been, what a show of light and colour across the ocean!), he visited his office and threw back a hefty whiskey, before going upstairs to change. Later, he managed to waylay Mrs. Hapgood as she tottered into the dining room. She was delighted at the news, and more than eager to change rooms as soon as possible.

The next morning, she said to Miss Chelmsford-Spruce, as they sat together in the back of the taxi taking them to church, 'That Mr. Channing is ever such a kind man. He's giving me a room on the first floor, so I do not have so far to climb.'

'That's very nice of him, Millicent,' Miss Chelmsford-Spruce responded. 'I hope you will not have trouble paying the increased rate.'

'Oh no,' said Mrs. Hapgood. 'He says he wont be increasing the rate. Isn't that kind of him, Mabel?'

'Yes, it is.'

And from that time forward, Mrs. Hapgood ceased to criticise Richard's and Antonia's closeness. Indeed, she was heard to come to their defence a few days later, when one of the other elderly permanent residents was casting doubts on the propriety of their relationship.

Chapter Sixteen

Richard met his wife, at her parents' instigation, at their home in Constantia one morning in early December. Richard had held out some small hopes that he might see Jeremy while he was there; however, Helen was alone in the drawing room of the large house (but for Skattie the Skippertjie dog, who was sitting on her lap, and who emitted two or three accusatory yaps at Richard as he entered the room).

'Richard,' Helen greeted him, having removed the dog from her lap and risen from the chair.

'Helen. How are you?'

'I'm well. How are you, Richard?'

It had been years since either had asked the other how they were.

Helen was looking, Richard acknowledged, simply lovely, with a flawless, glowing complexion – obviously, she had been spending much time in healthy outdoor pursuits, such as tennis and riding – and her golden hair was shining. She wore an outfit Richard did not remember having seen before, a dress of lawn (not that Richard would have known the material's name) with a dense, printed floral pattern in shades of pink and green. Her makeup and her jewellery were, for Helen, fairly restrained. Altogether, thought Richard, a very attractive package, but one which awoke in him less emotional attachment than might a very beautiful and very valuable Ming vase have done.

'I'm OK, Helen,' he answered her.

A Coloured maid brought some coffee to them on a tray, and placed the tray on a low table. They both sat down on opposite sides of the table, on which was a scattering of glossy magazines, a couple of marble ashtrays, and a large ceramic ornament. Skattie jumped up onto her mistress' lap again. Richard waited for his wife to speak; after all, he had not called this meeting. Helen was to be disappointed if she had been expecting Richard to commence the meeting with a plea for her return. So she occupied herself with pouring two coffees, one black. She passed the latter across the low table to Richard.

'I expect I'm as much at fault as you are, Richard,' she began. Fault!? thought Richard. I was not aware I was at fault! 'But I would like to try to make our marriage work.'

'Yes ... ?' Richard responded, his tone far from warm.

'Jeremy needs stability in his life.' Helen was stroking Skattie absently. 'He's going to be facing many new challenges now. I don't think our continued separation will do him any good.'

'I agree with you there,' Richard responded. 'But honestly, can we live together anymore? The evidence seems to indicate otherwise.'

Richard was amazed at how calm and controlled he felt. But then, he was determined not to come across as the supplicant in this exchange.

'We might make a few changes,' Helen replied. 'I've been thinking, we could have separate bedrooms.'

Richard was initially taken by surprise by the idea, but it took him only a few seconds' thought to realise that they would never anyway know an intimate relationship again, and that separate bedrooms would reduce the frequency with which they rubbed each other up the wrong way. (And he would not have to share his bed with Skattie ever again!) So he said, 'Actually, that might be a good idea.'

'We could keep our sitting room in common, somewhere we could come together,' Helen continued. Richard understood that she had thought this thing through. 'Many marriages work very well with separate bedrooms. But (and Helen's mouth acquired a stubborn set all too familiar to Richard), I want Antonia to go.'

'No,' Richard retorted. 'She can stay as long as she wishes.'

'Then, try and make it less obvious how smitten you are with her.'

Richard was beginning to feel angry. This was not going well anymore. He needed a drink. He could feel the hip flask in his trouser pocket. 'Smitten?' he responded. 'If by that you mean that I'm showing a welcome to my cousin – an innocent young girl!'

'Oh, Richard. It's obvious that you're very much taken by her!'

Richard drew a deep, long breath. Then he asked, 'Have you any other conditions?'

'No,' his wife replied. 'I would like to come back – if only for Jeremy's sake. But I do not wish to feel that I'm going to be in public competition with Antonia.'

'I will give you no cause to feel that Antonia and I are going to humiliate you publicly,' Richard assured his wife, 'but she's been through a rough time back home, and she doesn't deserve to be treated badly again.'

'Well ... we'll see,' Helen responded. 'I would like to move back after Jeremy has written his Matric exams. Sometime after mid-December. How does that seem to you?'

'Right,' Richard said. 'We'll try to make a go of it.' He had not touched his coffee in its delicate little bone china cup. He drank it down now in two quick gulps, then stubbed out the cigarette he had lighted a few minutes earlier. 'If you need help with anything in the meanwhile, let me know,' he continued. 'Otherwise, let me know when you're ready to come back. I'll have a separate bedroom prepared. Have you any preference?'

'Yes, I was thinking that you could move into the Blue Room.'

"My God," thought Richard, "she expects *me* to move! But then, why not?" He had never used their sitting room much (which adjoined with their bedroom); not as often as Helen had – he had his office downstairs, after all. He might as well change bedrooms. The Blue Room, on the first floor, had a sea view, and was one of only eight bedrooms in total on both the first and second floors with an *en suite* bathroom and lavatory. In his great-aunt's day, there had been only three *en suite* bedrooms in total; he had had the remaining five converted soon after deciding to run Pitlochry House as a hotel, while he had still had some funds to draw upon. Of the eight *en suite* bedrooms, he and Helen had shared one;

Jeremy had another permanently put aside for him; Miss Chelmsford-Spruce had a third; Mrs. Hapgood, despite her recent change of rooms, still had a fourth; Antonia had a fifth – and he would now be taking a sixth *en suite* bedroom. That would leave only two *en suite* bedrooms available right now for guests, thought Richard – and their busy season (such as it was) was almost upon them.

'Right-O,' Richard repeated, 'Let me know when you're ready to move back, and I'll have the rooms prepared.' He stood, and Helen stood also, the dog in her arms. They stared at each other for a moment, then Richard said, 'Until then. Goodbye, Helen.'

'Goodbye for now, Richard.'

Neither had shaken hands with the other.

Helen's father was waiting in the hallway as Richard left. 'I hope it went well,' he asked.

'Yes, it went quite well, Henry,' answered Richard. Henry Du Bois had been baptised "Hendrik," but he had anglicised his name.

'So my daughter will be returning to you?'

'Helen wants to come home, yes – once Jeremy has finished writing his Matric exams.'

'That's good. I'm glad.'

The two men shook hands, and Richard got into his car. Once in the car, he swallowed a hefty slug from his silver, leather bound hip flask. Then, starting the engine, he lighted another cigarette and pulled away.

Richard had a generous heart. As he drove home, he was thinking, "Helen was trying hard, I must give her that." When he got home, he entered the house past the kitchen and domestic offices, making haste to reach his office, with Katy (who had met him at the back door) trotting at his heels. He wished to be alone for a while, so that he could brood on the implications of his meeting with Helen. He met no one in the entrance hall, and was able to avoid having to greet anyone, and when he reached his office he made for his desk. Pulling open a drawer, he removed the bottle of Bushmills, along with a tumbler, and poured himself a very stiff whiskey, gulping it down in three quick swallows. Then he sat down in the big leather armchair, a newly lighted cigarette between his fingers.

He had a horrid feeling that a great deal of misery lay ahead of him.

Helen appeared to have acquired a great many more clothes during her absence. Her father, driving behind her in his Mercedes-Benz, unloaded several suitcases that would not fit into her small sports car. But at least Helen's return meant that Richard was able to see his son again. Jeremy accompanied his mother when she returned to Pitlochry House, and Richard shook his son's hand, and said, 'Welcome home, Jem.' Antonia had had the delicacy to absent herself from this occasion. She had taken Katy for a walk on the mountainside.

'Thanks Dad.'

'How did your exams go?' asked Richard.

'I think I did OK,' the boy replied.

'That's good. When will you have the results?'

'Later this month, Dad.'

'We'll keep our fingers crossed, then.'

At lunch that day, after Richard, Helen, Antonia and

Jeremy had sat down at table together, Antonia, smiling (determined to ignore the almost palpable air of tension she felt at their table, and trying hard to overcome the dislike she felt for Richard's wife), greeted Helen. 'Hullo Helen. It's nice to see you again.'

'Antonia. Has Richard been looking after you?'

'Oh yes. I'm enjoying my stay *so* much.'

'That's good. Marta!' Helen addressed the maid. 'Bring me another fork. This one's dirty.'

'Ja, Merrem.' The maid disappeared.

Antonia had a sinking feeling that problems lay ahead. But she *was* enjoying her stay, and she did not want to leave yet – certainly not at this time of year; she did not fancy returning to an England caught fast in midwinter's icy grip.

When Jeremy received his Matric examination results, he found he had done very well in all his subjects except History (and in that, he had still done well enough for his purposes). His father had always enjoyed History at school. Perhaps the pleasure Richard took in ancient structures, and in architecture, was linked to his enjoyment of History. These pleasures were absent in Jeremy – as they were absent in his mother. Jeremy was very much his mother's son. But it was Richard who insisted on taking him to one of Cape Town's oldest and most select gentlemen's outfitters, so that he could choose something to wear for his Matric Dance, which was to be held on the evening of Wednesday the 22nd. Helen showed that she was trying hard to make the reconciliation a success, and so she did not insist that she herself be the one to take Jeremy in to Cape Town.

At the outfitters, Jeremy's innate breeding came to the fore, and so he rejected various startling outfits in purple, magenta and pink, inspired by American high school graduation dances (as viewed on cinema screens and on the television), choosing instead a classic white tie and tails ensemble even more splendid than the one Richard still had hanging up somewhere (and which probably no longer fitted him). The outfit's trouser hems had not the least suggestion of a flare, although flared trousers were at that time ubiquitous. Wearing this costume, Jeremy looked extraordinarily handsome. His mother (who had coached him in the waltz, foxtrot, rumba and swing – those classic ballroom dances which would occupy the earlier part of the evening at his Matric Dance) saw him wearing it for the first time on the evening of the Dance itself.

'My beautiful boy!' Helen declared, and removing a tiny, lace-edged, embroidered and scented handkerchief from her bosom, she dabbed at her eyes. How much pleasure she took in her handsome, gifted son; how, on contemplating him, she was sometimes moved to expressions of bathetic sentiment ... for of course, Helen was hard as nails, and very little truly touched her deeply.

Jeremy cast his own eyes down modestly towards his expensive, fine leather Italian shoes. (Yes, his outfit incorporated beautifully made Italian dancing pumps which could never be used for walking any distance at all in, and which had cost Richard a fortune).

'My gosh, Jeremy!' exclaimed Antonia, who was passing through the hall as the boy came downstairs. 'You'll knock 'em dead!' Indeed, she thought that he looked like a young prince.

Jeremy grinned at her, and he and his father disappeared towards the back door and the garages.

They could still see the sun low above the sea's western horizon as they reached the crest of Silvermine, but the sun was long gone behind the mountains as they reached the school. On the way there, they had stopped off in Newlands, to collect Jeremy's date for the evening, a girl a year younger than himself, named Jenny, the sister of one of his school friends. Jeremy was fond of her, indeed, quite attracted to her – she was pretty enough in her terrace dress, after all – but he was by no means head over heels in love with her, and he was able to maintain just that touch of distance in their relationship which excited her to show greater interest in him than he showed for her. Jeremy was perfectly accustomed to girls showing a greater interest in him than he felt for them: he got quite a kick out of it. Jenny was tremendously keyed up and excited – she was only sixteen, and this was her first formal dance – and she talked incessantly during the short drive from her home to the school.

She wore a corsage consisting of a single yellow orchid with a spray of rosemary and lavender, which Jeremy had presented to her at her front door, where he had helped pin it to her bosom. Jeremy's mother had driven in to Fish Hoek that morning, where she had bought the corsage from the florist shop. She had kept it in damp cotton wool in one of the kitchen refrigerators, and had given it to Jeremy as he and his father had left for the Dance.

As Richard dropped the two of them off outside the school, he said, 'Enjoy yourselves, both of you. Try to avoid any illicit hooch, Jem.'

'Oh Dad, as if – !' (How embarrassing his father could be, how gauche! How Jeremy wished that he was old enough to drive. Roll on next April!).

'I'll be back at eleven,' Richard told them.

'OK. Bye, Dad,' and the boy got out of the car, went round to Jenny's door, and handed her out. Then the two disappeared up the driveway, in company with another young couple, who had been dropped off in a Mercedes-Benz car. (One of the things that Helen held against her husband was that they did not own a Mercedes-Benz car).

Richard had seen more of his son in the last few days than he had for a long time.

It was almost nine o' clock by the time Richard got back to Pitlochry House. He left the car (he was using the Ford) in front of the house, for in not much more than an hour's time, he would have to set off again. He filled in his time watching television in the residents' lounge. He drank two whiskeys while he was doing so. Helen's chair was drawn up alongside him, while Antonia was sharing a sofa with Mr. Carstairs, who, although it was out of character, was rather taken by the young woman. What were they all watching? No one would remember the next day: it was some silly American nonsense, instantly forgettable. But what was SABC to do, when Equity, the British actors' union, had placed an embargo on the export of British television programmes to the wicked Apartheid South Africa?

Richard was so accustomed to driving under the influence of liquor that his two large whiskeys posed him no problem on the night drive over the mountains after ten o' clock, nor on the drive through the suburbs that followed, with its several traffic lights and light traffic. And of course, he knew the route so well, each stop, twist and turn, that he could almost do it in his sleep. Which was fortunate, as on the way to the school he had almost dozed off behind the wheel on two occasions. But he woke up fully with his son's arrival at the car, Jenny on his arm. The boy's elegant outfit was somewhat dishevelled, with his waistcoat unbuttoned and his white bow tie draped loosely around his neck. (It was not a ready-tied bow tie, but a real tie, which Richard had had to tie for Jeremy). And judging from his speech, which was very slightly slurred, he had clearly partaken of some illicit alcohol. But he nonetheless opened the door for Jenny, and saw her seated, before getting into the car himself. Like his father, he remained a gentleman even when taken by drink. How could his father take him to task? Richard of all people could not remonstrate with his son for his inebriated condition. Instead he asked, 'Have you had a good time?'

'Yeah, Dad. It was fun.'

They dropped Jeremy's partner off at her home in Newlands, Jeremy kissing her goodnight at her front door. Neither Jeremy nor his father had much to say to each other during the long dark drive home, and after a while, Jeremy fell asleep. He awoke when the car reached Pitlochry House. Jeremy was not too keen on his mother (who had stayed up for them) embracing and kissing him; he knew that she would smell the liquor on him. But he could not prevent her from clasping him to her bosom, and sure enough, her nose wrinkling, she exclaimed, 'Oh Jeremy! You've been drinking.'

'Just a little, Mum. After all, I'm an adult now.'

'Well,' his mother responded, 'I suppose it was a special

occasion. You can tell me all about it tomorrow.' But Helen was afraid for her darling son; afraid that Richard's weakness for drink might one day express itself in Jeremy too. Alone but for her Skippertjie dog in her bedroom that night, her thoughts were not entirely restful ones.

Jeremy however, his mind free of any anxieties, slept the deep, untroubled, healthy sleep of youth.

Chapter Seventeen

There was a Christmas tree standing in the entrance hall, which Richard and Antonia had had fun decorating a day or two before Helen's return. They had had to use a step ladder, for the tree stood over nine feet tall, and dominated the hall. At the very top of the tree was a large silver star, which Richard, holding the step ladder for her, had got Antonia to fix in place.

'Hold the ladder steady, Richard,' she said with a nervous laugh.

'I've got you!'

She reached up and on her third attempt, managed to stick the star on the topmost point of the tree.

'Well done!' said Richard. Antonia beamed down at him. Oh, how loveable she was!

On the morning of Christmas Day, in the privacy of Richard's office, he and Antonia exchanged gifts. Antonia gave Richard a beautifully illustrated book on Western Cape vernacular architecture, which she had found at the CNA in Fish Hoek, and Richard gave Antonia a very fine, framed watercolour of the main façade of Pitlochry House, painted some years earlier by his artist friend, John.

'Oh, Richard, that's a lovely present! It will bring back happy memories for me no matter how old I grow.'

Richard leant forward and kissed her on the mouth. This was their first real kiss since Helen's return. 'I want you to remember us,' he said, stepping back a pace after a short while. 'I know I will never forget you.'

It seemed to each of them that this magic interlude, this extended time out of Time which was Antonia's visit to Pitlochry House, was drawing to a close, even though neither of them had any conscious plans as yet to end it.

It was a real scorcher of a day, with the temperature in the shade reaching almost ninety degrees Fahrenheit by lunchtime. Some of the old ladies had gathered in the entrance hall shortly before lunchtime to admire the tree and chat among themselves, their happy memories of Christmases long ago (some reaching back to distant childhoods) rekindled. Richard had also hung a Christmas garland on the front door. But these were the only Christmas decorations he had put up. Four of the residents were spending Christmas Day with relatives, but the remaining five residents, along with the Channings and Antonia, and two non-resident couples with three children between them (who had booked their Christmas lunches at Pitlochry House Hotel) – sixteen people in all – would be seated at the big mahogany dining table, which was fifteen feet long and five feet wide. It was laid with starched white table cloths, and in the centre of the table was placed a big, gleaming copper basin, in which was arranged a large floral display made up primarily of King Protea blooms gathered from the mountainside near the house. At one end of the dining room, against the wall between the two doors which gave access to the entrance hall, stood a massive, highly polished, carved sideboard and dresser of European oak darkened with age, with tall silver candlesticks at either end, and an impressive display of Spode dinnerware arranged above the wide serving top.

At each place setting was a paper party hat, which almost everyone, even Helen, in whom Antonia had never observed any marked spirit of fun, and the adolescent Jeremy – who usually strove hard to avoid appearing younger than he was – now donned. Miss Chelmsford-Spruce and Mrs. Hapgood, however, were wearing their church-going hats, and they refused to remove them. There was a large, gaudy Christmas cracker also at each place setting, and Antonia thought the children's parents might have a job to stop them being pulled immediately. 'No, Robert,' one of the mothers was already addressing the eldest of her two little boys, who, with his brother, had already seized one of the crackers. 'You must wait until the pudding course.'

Marta, wearing a black dress and black stockings, with a freshly starched white cap and apron, with André (wearing his white jacket and black bow tie) walking behind her, came in bearing a silver tray on which were two bottles of wine, both of which had been opened. Richard immediately took charge of one of the bottles of Nederburg Sauvignon Blanc, while André (who was serving, as this was such a special occasion, as a butler for this meal) went round the dining table pouring wine from the bottle's twin for those who wished it.

Richard filled the smaller of his three wine glasses (impressively expansive individual place settings had been laid on this great feast day, a mass of gleaming silver and sparkling glassware), and raised it to his lips, rapidly reducing the level by about an inch and a half. There were a number of jugs of water, along with some small bottles of carbonated apple juice on the table, for those diners who did not wish to drink wine. The carbonated apple juice proved popular with the children.

It was Helen who was responsible for the beautiful and impressive appearance of the dining table. Indeed, as she was good at this sort of occasion, she had arranged the entire Christmas lunch.

Richard saw that everyone now had a glass either of wine, apple juice, or water, in front of them, and he pushed back his chair and stood up, raising his own glass of wine and wishing his guests and family a happy Christmas. 'And an especially warm Christmas to Antonia, whose first Christmas in Africa this is,' he added.

'Hear-hear!' seconded Jeremy (how grown up he was), smiling at Antonia.

The soup course (of which the children were rather wary, for it was spicy and strong) comprised cold *gazpacho*, and was followed by grilled *kabeljou* fillets. Both the young mothers present, thinking ahead to the main and desert courses, did not insist that the children eat any of the fish.

But Antonia thought the fish was delicious. 'This fish is wonderful, Helen,' she declared. 'What is it?'

Helen responded with a rather brittle smile. She was trying as hard to be pleasant as Antonia was. '*Kabeljou*,' she answered, pronouncing the word "cubblejoe," as if its Afrikaans pronunciation was alien to her. 'They were fresh from Hout Bay late yesterday afternoon, and Elsbet kept them refrigerated overnight.'

As each course was finished, the empty bowls and plates were removed by Marta and Bella. Antonia chatted for a while with Miss Grogan, who was seated to her right. Helen was engaged in conversation with one of the other elderly guests, and Richard was chatting with Miss Chelmsford-Spruce. Jeremy, who was seated to Antonia's left, managed to make them both laugh as he broke into her conversation with Miss Grogan, and recounted some amusing incident from the recent Matric Dance. Then he asked Antonia, 'Would you like to come swimming at Fish Hoek beach tomorrow? It's going to be another scorcher.'

The young English woman hesitated for a moment. Richard was staring at the two of them. 'OK,' she answered, 'That would be nice.'

'Cool!' Jeremy exclaimed. 'Mum will probably drop us off.' He was wondering whether Antonia would be wearing a bikini, or a one piece bathing suit. He was sure there would be people he knew there, to admire his taste in girls. But Antonia now began speaking across the table to one of the luncheon visitors, who, with her husband and little girl, was seated across from her. (It transpired that they were on holiday from the Transvaal, and so they could not celebrate Christmas lunch at home). Jeremy therefore applied himself silently to his meal and to his wine. (His mother had permitted him to begin drinking wine with his meals a year earlier).

Richard was now on his third glass of white wine, and the main course had yet to commence. Then two roast turkeys were brought in by the serving girls, who strained under the weight of the giant birds. (What the guests did not eat, the servants would, cold, that evening and the following day. Elsbet would use the carcasses to add flavour and body to the turkey consommé she proposed making, which she would serve for the soup course at dinner tomorrow). Richard, seated at the head of the long table, began carving one of the birds (with Marta and Bella stationed just behind and on either side of him, ready to begin serving the fruits of his labours around the table). There were heaps of golden baked potatoes in serving bowls, along with carrots and parsnips (both these latter halved lengthwise, dipped in honey, and caramelized in the oven), and fresh peas, baked onions, and pork, sage and onion stuffing. The children's eyes were almost popping out of their heads at this plenty. Mr. Carstairs, who, despite being thin as a rake, could eat like a horse, felt himself salivating. He dabbed at his lips with his linen napkin.

Richard beckoned André closer, and spoke to him. André then instructed one of the maids to fetch a bottle of Constantia Pinot Noir from the kitchen pantry.

'Turkey needs a red wine,' Richard announced. 'I'm right, aren't I, Helen?'

'So they say,' Helen replied, 'but do we really need more wine?' But Richard poured a glass – the glass rather larger than the white wine glass – for himself.

'Who else would like some red wine with their turkey?' he asked.

'I think I will,' declared Miss Chelmsford-Spruce, presenting the second of the three wine glasses with which each place setting was furnished. Richard filled the glass, and passed it to the old lady. 'Your good health!' he pronounced, and raised his own glass.

Some of the guests accepted second helpings of the turkey. By then Richard was on his second glass of the Constantia red (that is to say, his fifth glass of wine). He was louder now than he had been at the beginning of the meal, but then, so were most of the other diners.

Helen alone among the diners had grown more silent. Helen, who had done so much in planning and choreographing this Christmas lunch, did not appear to be thoroughly enjoying herself. She would probably have been far happier celebrating Christmas at her parents' home, with her son present, than having to observe how much Richard and Antonia were enjoying themselves. The one saving grace, in Helen's view, was that Antonia was seated some distance from Richard – and right next to Jeremy.

The big Christmas pudding, its surface seeming to undulate with blue flame, was brought in by Marta. There were exclamations of delight from all three children, and from some of the old ladies too. Bella, instructed by André, went and fetched two bottles of Robertson Winery sparkling wine from the pantry, one of which Richard directed be placed in front of him. He removed first the foil and then the wire retainer from the top of the bottle and worked the cork up with his thumb, and there was a loud "pop!" followed by laughter, as the sparkling wine under pressure erupted from the bottle. Showing amazing quick thinking in one of fairly advanced years, Miss Chelmsford-Spruce thrust her wide champagne bowl (the third of the three wine glasses with which each place setting was furnished) towards him, and Richard caught the frothing wine in her glass, before passing it back to her. 'Who else is for some shampers?' he asked. The bottle, and then, once it too had been opened, the second bottle, were brought around the table by André to those who wished to join Richard and Miss Chelmsford-Spruce in the South African version of Champagne. There were many takers.

Young Robert and his brother had begun to pull as many Christmas crackers between them as they could lay their hands on. These included their parents' crackers, and those of the old ladies nearest them. The little girl, sitting with her parents across the table, joined in, as first her mother, then her father, seized hold of the other end of a cracker with her. "Crack – crack – crack!" The explosions were puny compared with the popping of corks from the sparkling wine, but the children began to laugh and even, once or twice, to shriek.

Antonia, young enough still to remember her own childhood vividly, felt quite at home amidst the noise and excitement. She turned to Jeremy and said, 'Let's pull a cracker!' Jeremy found a miniature spirit level inside the Christmas cracker, and he laid it on the dining table and laughingly informed Antonia that the table was not quite level. Antonia joined in his laughter.

Richard thoroughly approved of the bold pudding. In a stubborn recollection of his boyhood, he still found it difficult to exercise restraint when faced with sweet, gooey confections and plump, unctuous puddings. He was a big man, with big appetites. He found the brandy butter (which

Elsbet had prepared with KWV brandy from the Cape) to be especially delicious. The willowy Mr. Carstairs and the two little boys joined Richard and Jeremy in tucking eagerly into their wholesome Christmas pudding and brandy butter, but two of the old ladies, along with Helen and Antonia, chose instead the fruit salad with ice cream, as did the little girl. The two bottles of sparkling wine were soon emptied. Many of the old ladies were giggling by now, although few of them got the point of the silly jokes inside the remaining Christmas crackers (those that had thus far survived the children's attention), which were now being pulled by momentary partnerships between the guests.

Inside the old house, shaded by its wide veranda, and with its high ceilings and thick walls, it was pleasantly cool, but beyond the deep, covered veranda, the African sun of high summer beat down. Perhaps the sole concession made to the Cape Town midsummer heat had been the cold *gazpacho* soup with which the Christmas lunch had begun. The meal itself was otherwise not very different at all (thought Antonia) to the Christmas lunches being consumed that day in an England caught fast in the icy grip of midwinter. However, the diners were afterwards served their coffees outside on the shaded veranda, where there was a stirring of air. Seated comfortably in cushioned wicker chairs, several of them before long (including Richard, who had accompanied his coffee with two shot glasses of the Drambuie liqueur that Mrs. Hapgood had given him) had dozed off. Jeremy, however (even making allowances for his young man's prodigious appetite), had ate a little more than was wise, so he found a chair with a cushion in it at the far end of the long, deep veranda, away from the others, and sat back in the chair, folding his hands across his somewhat distended stomach. He closed his eyes and within five minutes he too had fallen asleep.

Chapter Eighteen

Despite the proximity of the sea, Antonia had not yet gone bathing. The truth is, Richard, for all his love of boats and the sea, was not very fond of sea bathing. On Boxing Day morning, Helen gave the two young people a lift to Fish Hoek in the Ford Granada. Richard stood watching from the veranda as they set off, a frown on his face. Both youngsters were in high spirits – Antonia because of happy childhood memories of seaside holidays, and Jeremy because of his having gained the uncontested company of this lovely young woman. Once in Fish Hoek they crossed the Cape Peninsula railway line at the level crossing just before reaching the beach, and Helen pulled up in the car park.

'What time would you like me to fetch you both?' she asked. Jeremy glanced at his wristwatch: it was now eleven o' clock.

'How about three o' clock, Mum?' he suggested.

'OK. Enjoy yourselves,' Helen said, and pulled away. She was glad to see Antonia spending time with Jeremy, rather than with her husband; perhaps her son would succeed in alienating the girl's affections for Richard?

Both the young people were already wearing their swimming costumes. Jeremy's bathing costume comprised baggy, bright yellow swimming trunks. He wore a tee-shirt printed with a portrait of Jim Morrison (who had died five years earlier) of *The Doors*, and he carried a towel. Antonia carried a small leather shoulder bag, in which were a few personal necessities, including also Jeremy's wallet for safe keeping. She wore her one piece lime green bathing costume (Jeremy was not overly disappointed: she still looked stunning in it, he soon decided) beneath a pair of shorts and a tee-shirt. She had a light cotton hat on her head. Both she and Jeremy were wearing sandals. The beach, which shone white in the hot sun, was crowded with visitors, many of them up-country holiday makers. There was, of course, not a black or a Coloured face to be seen – with one exception: this was the Coloured man selling ice creams in the car park from a small handcart, protected from the sun by a candy-striped canopy. Except at its extreme northern end (and bereft of any facilities), Fish Hoek bathing beach was accessible only to whites – as signboards located at intervals along the edge of the beach proclaimed: "Whites Only – *Net Blanke*."

'Where can I change?' Antonia asked.

'I'll show you the changing rooms,' Jeremy replied, and they set off. He stood and waited outside while Antonia stripped off the pair of shorts and the tee-shirt she wore over her bathing costume, placing them in her bag. Then they headed up the beach for one hundred yards, before spreading their towels on the sand. Jeremy now removed his tee-shirt. Unlike the English girl, whose limbs – despite several hikes in the mountains, and a day's sailing with Richard – were still rather pale, Jeremy had a golden tan. He was certainly very good looking, thought Antonia: broad shouldered, like his father, he had the slim waist, narrow hips, and long legs of an athlete – and to be sure, he had always done well at sports at school. His short hair was far fairer than Antonia's honey-blonde hair. They made a very attractive couple, the picture of youthful good looks and good health. Indeed, they might have been taken for brother and sister.

'Race you!' declared Jeremy, and set off at a lope for the water's edge. Antonia followed at a run, and overtook the boy (who had allowed her to do so, so that he could admire her trim and shapely form from behind). The sea was very calm, with only small wavelets breaking in the low surge and ebb of the water. It was, unusually for this time of year, an almost windless day. As soon as the water had reached Jeremy's waist, he flung himself face-forward and began to head out in a crawl. Antonia was happy however just to remain bobbing up and down in the gentle swell, the water rarely reaching much further than her waist. But after a while, she too flung herself face-forward – how cold the water felt! – and she doggy paddled just hard enough to hold her place against the incoming swell. She could not see Jeremy, but after a while he reappeared, and stood up, scattering shining water droplets, and splashed her, grinning. Antonia splashed him back, laughing. After a few more minutes of play in the water they headed back up the beach to their towels. Antonia donned her floppy cotton hat.

'Do you mind if I call you Tony?' Jeremy asked the girl.
'Sure, many of my friends do,' Antonia replied.

'My friends call me Jem,' Jeremy volunteered.

'OK, Jem,' Antonia smiled at him.

As they sat in the sun, the salt quickly drying on their skin, they chatted, sharing stories about their respective backgrounds, and about the music they liked. Both agreed that *Pink Floyd* was "amazing." Jeremy was also a fan of the *Rolling Stones*, while Antonia preferred the *Beatles*. Both the youngsters thought that the fairly recently deceased and beatified Jim Morrison, and his group, *The Doors*, were "incredible."

'I've visited his grave, you know,' remarked Antonia.

'Really? That's cool! Where is he buried?'

'In the *Cimetière du Père-Lachaise* in Paris,' Antonia responded.

'Do you know Paris?' Jeremy asked.

'Yeah, I've visited a few times.'

'You're lucky,' Jeremy commented. 'We're such a long way from anywhere, here in South Africa. But I'll travel someday.'

After a while they lay flat on their towels, and lay in companionable silence, basking in the sun.

At about half past noon, Jeremy sat up and suggested they cool off in the water again, before going to get something to eat. Refreshed from their second dip in the ocean, Jeremy (having pulled on his Jim Morrison tee-shirt and taken charge of his wallet) led Antonia (who had wrapped her towel, sarong fashion, around her waist) to the cafeteria, where he paid for hamburgers and milkshakes for the two of them. ("No, no, it's my treat, Tony," he had insisted, when Antonia had attempted to pay for her food).

Humanity in all its variety was on show in the cafeteria: there was a scattering of elderly folk, some of them more akin to lizards in appearance than to Human beings, with wrinkled skin as brown as old leather from years of avid sun-worship. There were several families with young children, and in one corner there were two tables pushed together, at which young people Antonia's and Jeremy's ages sat. Jeremy made for this group, and there was a round of greetings. He clearly knew most of these youngsters.

'This is Antonia, who's visiting from England,' Jeremy told the group.

A chorus of "*Howzit*, Antonia," arose from the gathering, and room was made for the two of them to sit down with their trays. No one was smoking; no one was drinking liquor; what a healthy, tanned, glowing gathering of young people this was!

Jeremy and Antonia went for one more (somewhat abbreviated) dip in the sea after lunch, then, still wearing their bathing costumes, they sluiced off under the cold water outdoor showers, open to the public gaze, located outside the changing rooms block. Thereafter, Jeremy led the young English girl along the beach towards the Catwalk, a narrow paved pathway that twisted and wound its way just above the rocky shoreline at the southern end of the beach. They found an unclaimed bench alongside the pathway to sit on, and Jeremy removed his tee-shirt again, catching the strong afternoon sun on his body. Once in a while a commuter train, powered by an overhead electric cable, would rumble by just behind them, only a few feet further up the slope.

Jeremy broke their silence. 'Do you have a boyfriend waiting for you in England, Tony?'

There was a pause, then Antonia replied, 'No. Not anymore.'

Jeremy intuited that this topic was better not pursued, and they lapsed into silence again. Indeed, Antonia thought that Jeremy might have fallen into a doze. She looked sideways at him. His eyes were closed against the sun. There was an almost feline air of satisfaction about him. What flawless, golden skin he had! How smooth the muscles on his torso were! "Dont go there," Antonia thought. She turned back and stared at the sparkling blue waters of the bay, remembering her sail with Richard. That had been a happy day.

It was almost three o' clock. Jeremy opened his eyes and looked at his wristwatch. 'Mum will be here soon,' he said. 'We'd better go.'

Jeremy's mother had not yet arrived. He bought them each an ice cream cone. They sat on a low wall, trying to eat their ice creams faster than the sun was melting them, and Helen pulled up in the car.

'You look like you two had a good time,' she commented, as they stood up and threw the remains of their ice cream cones into a nearby rubbish bin.

'*Ja*, we did,' Jeremy responded. 'Didn't we, Tony?'

'I enjoyed myself,' the girl agreed, smiling at Jeremy.

Helen noted with approval her son's use of the diminutive for Antonia's name: it would be good if Antonia was bonding with her son. 'I hope you don't peel,' she remarked to the English girl, whose limbs had certainly caught a great deal of sun. But over the next few days Antonia's skin did not peel; instead, she began to look less like a visitor from the northern hemisphere, and more like a native Capetonian. Jeremy thought she looked wonderful.

Richard had spent his time sulking, and drinking in his office, before taking Katy for a walk. On his return he sat on the veranda, joining the residents, who were already gathering in anticipation of tea, cakes, sandwiches and social intercourse. (The three meals of the day, along with morning and afternoon tea, constituted tremendously important landmarks in the residents' daily lives, and they looked forward to them eagerly). Thus it was that Richard witnessed Antonia's cheerful return with his son. He told himself that he should not resent her having a good time with someone her own age once in a while. But it would have been easier for the besmitten Richard to bear had it not been his own son with whom Antonia had been enjoying herself. How ignoble and demeaning jealousy is!

Chapter Nineteen

Every New Year's Eve the Pitlochry House Hotel held a dinner-dance. Richard's and Helen's personal guests, along with the hotel residents, sat at the big table in the dining room. The dinner served at this table was a four course meal – with plenty of wine – to a set menu. Tickets to the dance were sold at several outlets in Fish Hoek during the preceding two weeks, or by telephone bookings, and on the evening itself, by a senior school pupil from Fish Hoek High School stationed behind a table just inside the entrance hall. Extra tables seating four people each, and hired from a catering outfit for the purpose, were arranged around the perimeter of the great hall (in which the dance was held), and on the long, deep veranda. Visitors seated on the veranda – the overspill from the dining room, which had a number of individual tables arranged in it, in addition to the big communal table in the centre of the room – could order from a menu featuring a small selection of three course dinners (if they intended eating at all. Many would order only drinks). The great hall, that enormous room reaching through two stories in height, with its minstrel gallery at one end of the room, high above the dancers, and the two cavernous fireplaces (whose wide grates were filled at this time of the year with displays of dried pine cones and dried King Proteas), provided a dramatic setting for the dance. The Pitlochry House Hotel's New Year's Eve dance was known throughout the region, and was very popular. Few of its competitors in and around Cape Town could provide as dramatic a setting for their New Year's Eve dances. Richard habitually wore a dinner jacket and black tie the night of the dinner-dance. This year, his son would be wearing his elegant white tie and tails outfit, and would (his mother was certain) outshine all the other men present. Helen was planning to wear an evening gown of pale blue silk, with a lot of expensive jewellery on display.

Skattie the Skippertjie dog would be consigned to Helen's bedroom for the evening, and traditionally, Skattie would wee on Helen's bedroom floor, even though the hotel's man-of-all-work, Charlie, would have taken her into the garden just before dinner. Katy, however, would be prohibited only the dining room during dinner, and could otherwise wander freely during the evening, for she was popular with the guests, and she did not become over-excited in a crowd.

Of the clothes that Antonia had packed before leaving England, the most appropriate outfit for the evening (she thought) was a cocktail dress, also of silk, in a daring cherry red. Only a very pretty younger woman such as Antonia could carry such an outfit off. She would be wearing the one piece of good jewellery she had with her – the big gold locket with its heavy gold chain – around her neck. Both Richard and Jeremy gaped in admiration when they saw her:

she looked stunning! (And, thought Jeremy, the lush, bold colour of her dress made her look a little bit naughty, and he could certainly live with that).

Richard, Helen, Jeremy and Antonia sat together with the Channings' personal guests and the hotel's residents at the big table in the dining room at dinner (a rather early dinner, to free Elsbet and her team – which included extra hired hands – to cope with the meals for the dance guests through the course of the evening). Most of the residents had dressed up for the evening, although only three or four of the old ladies, and of course, Mr. Carstairs, would actually hope to dance the first few numbers, which would be classic ballroom dances.

'Now remember, Jeremy, if you see any of the old dears sitting on the sidelines,' Richard had instructed his son (two tables had been reserved at the perimeter of the dance floor for the hotel residents to sit and watch the dance), 'ask whether they would like to dance, and stick to something they would recognise, something approaching a waltz – or if they're up to it, perhaps a foxtrot.'

'OK Dad.'

So between the two Channing men (and Mr. Carstairs, who considered himself an excellent ballroom dancer), the few elderly lady residents who were hoping to dance, were all able to enjoy a dance with a nicely dressed gentleman. Mr. Carstairs, in his dark suit, was indeed an elegant dancer. But not as elegant and attractive as the young Channing boy, in his white tie and tails.

'Doesn't Jeremy look just like Fred Astaire, Poppy?' Miss Chelmsford-Spruce asked Miss Grogan.

'Yes indeed,' Miss Grogan replied, 'but not as effeminate.'

'Oh really, Poppy!' responded Miss Chelmsford-Spruce. 'You should not say such things.'

'Why not, Mabel? I've never been afraid to call a shovel a spade.'

But Richard (who had had two large whiskeys since the end of the early dinner, along with several glasses of wine during dinner, and was as a consequence no longer entirely sober – not that anyone who did not know him would ever have guessed) approached Miss Chelmsford-Spruce when the next dance began, and she was thrilled to be asked to dance by the hotel's handsome proprietor. She was dressed up to the nines, in a dark blue velvet evening gown (which was altogether too heavy for the climate at this time of year), with some sparkling diamonds at her throat, and the usual collection of jewelled rings on her fingers. Miss Grogan was more sensibly apparelled, in a sateen dress reaching just below the midway point of her calves, and it was Jeremy (pleasingly lacking in effeminacy as he was) who invited her to dance. But Antonia had been Jeremy's first dance partner of the evening (for Jeremy had not invited a girl to the dinner-dance: he had wanted an unimpeded run at Antonia), and Jeremy was looking forward to being able to ask her again. When the dance ended, Jeremy smiled and inclined his head to Miss Grogan, and went to see if he could find Antonia, who seemed to have disappeared. Perhaps she was on the veranda?

The small tables that had been arranged around the perimeter of the dance floor were occupied with people drinking, chatting animatedly during the breaks, listening to the live music, and watching the dancers. The kitchen would soon be closing. It was warm even in the huge, high ceilinged room. There was a constant movement of people between the tables and the dance floor – and through the French windows onto the veranda also, as they sought some fresh air. There were still some new arrivals too, and cars were now parked some distance down the edge of the driveway, leaving only just enough room on the narrow road for vehicles to pass by very slowly. The night sky was clear. Those couples who descended the veranda steps to take a turn in the open air (and perhaps to seek a moment of privacy in the garden), and there were several such couples, could see the sky above the distant ocean strewn thickly with stars. The moon had not yet risen.

Antonia was standing on the veranda, gazing out into the night, her hands resting on the balustrade. It was strange: during her visit to Cape Town she had not felt homesick before, but just a moment ago, a tremendous wave of homesickness had overwhelmed her, and driven her from the crowd and noise of the great hall. Could it be, perhaps, that she was finally over the boy in England who had hurt her so badly? Was it time to go home?

The music for one of the dances had just come to an end. The band was collectively mopping its faces and having a drink of water. Helen Channing was led back to one of the small tables at the edge of the dance floor by her partner of the moment – who happened to be Charles Van Der Poel. (The Van Der Poels were among the dozen or so personal guests invited to the dinner-dance by the Channings). Since her return to Pitlochry House in mid December, Helen had avoided Charles; she really had been determined to try to make her marriage work, but now, with this big, excessively masculine brute of a man holding her by the arm (Charles Van Der Poel, Helen thought, looked like one of the very dangerous big cats – who just happened to be dressed up in a dinner jacket), Helen was shaken by the sudden onset of lust.

There are some women who do not find kind, gentle men pleasing: they want to be dominated, even abused, at the hands of large, brutish men. Helen had realised long ago that she was just such a woman, and Richard simply was not up to the job. Large he was (it was his size that had first given rise to Helen's interest in him), but he was too much of a gentleman for Helen's sexual tastes. (Poor Richard: had he only known of this on their wedding night, he might have elicited more of a response from his bride).

'Let's go out to the veranda,' Helen suggested to Charles. The two of them left via one of the French windows opening onto the veranda; Sonia Van Der Poel was just about to begin another dance with a mutual Channing – Van Der Poel acquaintance.

Jeremy had found Antonia standing alone at the edge of the veranda, peering out at the night sky. 'Hullo,' he said. ''Are you feeling OK? I wondered where you had got to.'

Antonia looked around, and was about to say something like, "I needed to be alone for a while," when Jeremy suddenly seized hold of her and said, 'Come on, let's have another dance,' and kissed her, holding her so close to him that she began to struggle to break free from his grasp. At that moment, Richard too, accompanied by Katy the dog, stepped out onto the veranda from the entrance hall, and looking around, he saw Antonia clearly struggling in the arms of his son – who was assaulting her with kisses, the horrible boy.

Richard, suddenly consumed with hot jealousy and rage, yelled at his son, 'Let go of her! What do you think you're doing?' Jeremy released Antonia, and Richard strode up to the two of them. Antonia had stepped back two paces from Jeremy, who now received a resounding slap from his father on the side of his face. Helen, who had just taken in the scene, gave a little shriek, and her husband turned around, and saw her with Charles Van Der Poel. 'And you!' Richard shouted at her, 'Get away from that man!'

Had the light been bright enough on the veranda, it might have been seen how white (except for the mark of his father's hand on the side of his face) Jeremy's face had gone, and how red with anger Helen's face had instantly become.

'How dare you!' she shrieked. Others on the veranda had now turned to observe the drama. 'How dare you hit my son! And how dare you tell me what to do!'

Consumed by whiskey-fuelled anger, Richard (who was not quite the fool that his wife had thought him to be, and had for some while felt a faint suspicion that Helen's friendship with Sonia masked an untoward interest in Charles Van Der Poel) strode fast towards the two of them, and drawing his arm back, he swung his fist, his shoulder behind the swing, and punched Charles hard on the jaw. The big man staggered back several paces, a hand going to his jaw, and he stared with amazement at his host, then, stepping forward, he too swung a fist, which connected with

Richard's jaw. Snarling, Katy leapt for Charles Van Der Poel and grabbed the offending arm in her powerful jaws.

How speedily the evening had descended into shock and outrage!

Chapter Twenty

With the intervention of Jeremy (the boy was amazingly quick thinking, considering that he was still mentally reeling from the slap his father had given him), and that of a nearby acquaintance of the Channings (who poured his cold beer on top of the snarling dog's head), and with Richard's belated help also, Katy the dog was hauled off by the collar, and was prevented from doing Charles Van Der Poel any lasting damage – although the right sleeve of his dinner jacket would never look the same again. How fortunate that Skattie had been exiled for the evening: imagine the mayhem had the little dog joined in the excitement! Richard dragged the still growling dog inside, and hauled her by main force down the corridor to his office, where he closed her inside the room. He then returned to the scene of the engagement, where he observed Antonia standing on the sidelines, a look of shock on her face. Jeremy had joined his mother; he could not recall his father ever having struck him before.

Sonia, whom some kind soul had informed of the fracas, had rushed out from the great hall to join her husband on the veranda. Indeed, a small crowd of onlookers, eager for excitement, had by now gathered at the scene.

'The damn dog savaged me!' exclaimed Charles Van Der Poel to his wife, holding out his tattered sleeve, from within which drops of blood dripped. An onlooker offered Sonia his large handkerchief.

'Make a tourniquet,' he advised her. 'Here – !' He took back his handkerchief and rolled it up tight, and tied it around Charles' forearm just in front of the elbow.

The Van Der Poels left in a hurry, before Helen could return with the first aid kit and some bandages she had gone to fetch. She knew that these items were located somewhere behind Mrs. Stoddart's desk: it took her a while to find them. The Van Der Poels were headed for False Bay Hospital at Fish Hoek, there to celebrate their New Year's Eve, while Charles received the medical care and shots that Sonia insisted her husband required. Richard, feeling suddenly rather faint, not to mention dizzy (not only had he been drinking almost without let since the late afternoon, but Charles Van Der Poel had managed to land a real humdinger of a return blow on his jaw, before Katy's outraged intervention had ended the conflict), now returned to his office, where (with a now much calmer Katy lying on the floor alongside him) he had collapsed onto the daybed. There he spent the night, a tartan rug pulled across his legs. A wave of shame and misery almost left him eviscerated when, waking some time after breakfast, the previous night's events came rushing back to him. He had really alienated his son's regard now!

Richard did not see Helen taking off in her sports car, which was laden with as much luggage as could be squeezed into it – which was not much. By her side sat Jeremy, Skattie the dog held on his lap. (Jeremy's grandfather would arrive within a day or two, feeling somewhat embarrassed, to load the rest of their things into his car. Richard would direct Marta and Bella to help him).

Right now, Richard's head hurt, and his jaw ached, and his mouth felt horribly dry. His hands were trembling slightly, and he did not feel well. He found the bottle of Bushmills in the desk drawer and poured a hefty slug into one of the two tumblers he kept there, and gulped it down, then sat and smoked a cigarette. What he really needed was a large amount of water, and a couple of aspirin, followed by a strong coffee, and to obtain these things, he would have to leave the sanctuary of his office … He was not in the mood to engage with anyone this morning – at least, not until the whiskey had begun to do its work, and not until he had had a strong coffee – so he crept through the entrance hall and down the corridor past the staircase, headed for the kitchen, where he found two of Elsbet's kitchen maids, washing up the breakfast things. (There was of course no one on desk duty in the hall to witness Richard's sorry condition, this first day of January nineteen seventy-seven, although Jack, the University of Cape Town student who manned the reception desk – and performed a variety of other tasks – in the mornings during the university break in December and January – the only two months of the year when there was someone officially on mornings duty at the reception desk – would be back at his post in a few days' time).

'Morning,' Richard greeted the girls. He could not remember their names. He addressed the nearer of the two. 'Bring a black coffee – a strong black coffee – to my bedroom, please.'

'*Ja, Meneer,*' the girl (she was barely sixteen years old) replied. 'Uh ... where is your bedroom, *Meneer?*' The kitchen maids rarely if ever had any business in the rest of the house.

'Oh – make me the coffee now, and I'll take it up myself. OK?'

'*Ja, Meneer.*'

In due course, Richard made his way up the servants' staircase at the back of the house, and so to his bedroom, where he drank the coffee and smoked another cigarette, then he removed his sorry evening dress and shaved, took a shower, and changed into clean clothes. He needed to find someone who could tell him whether Helen and Jeremy were still around (but he did not wish to talk to either in person just yet), although he was fairly sure that they would have left this morning. When he came downstairs again, this time via the main staircase, feeling physically somewhat improved (he had taken two aspirin and drunk two glasses of water), there was no one in the hallway other than Katy, who joined him, her tail wagging as he knuckled the top of her furry head; there was no one in the great hall either, and the residents' lounge was also empty. On the veranda however were Mrs. Hapgood, Miss Chelmsford-Spruce, and a number of other residents, enjoying the morning fresh air and a chat. A silence descended on the group as Richard appeared. He ignored them, for he could see Antonia a little distance away, sitting near the balustrade. He joined her, but he did not sit down. Katy was eager for a walk.

'I made a bit of a scene last night,' he said.

The young woman looked a touch embarrassed.

'I apologise,' he continued. 'I overreacted.'

'There's no need to apologise, Richard,' Antonia replied. 'Perhaps we should try to forget all about it.'

'I don't suppose you know what has happened to my wife and son?' Richard asked.

'I heard that they left just after breakfast, in Helen's car. They had suitcases and the dog with them.'

'Oh, God, I really have done it now. Will Jeremy ever forgive me?'

The situation was all rather beyond Antonia's thus far somewhat limited experience of life, and she did not know what to say, so she remained silent.

'I love the boy, you know,' Richard continued.

'I know you do. Jeremy must know that, too,' Antonia responded. Richard sat down across the small table from her. 'Richard,' Antonia continued, having to force herself to meet his eye, for she was fully cognisant of the impact her announcement would have, 'I think it's time I went home. I'm feeling homesick. Do you know, I've been away for over six months!'

And this was true: Antonia was feeling homesick, even if the sensation was newly minted. And she had been away from home for a long time. At the age of eighteen, six months is a very long time indeed.

But at this news, a dark vision of loneliness, of being left all alone, with no one to love or to be loved by, no one to care for, assailed Richard, and he almost groaned aloud. Instead, he said, 'If that's what you want to do, Antonia.

As soon as the businesses open on Tuesday, we can make a booking for your flights home.'

It was now Saturday.

'Yes, that would be a good idea.' Antonia met Richard's eye. 'But I will always be grateful for your welcome, Richard, and for everything you have done for me.'

Richard managed a brave smile, and said, 'We did have some good times, didn't we?'

'Of course we did!' Antonia too managed a smile.

Standing up, Richard said, 'I must take Katy for a walk. I'll see you later.'

Katy and her master descended the veranda steps.

Antonia felt terribly sorry for Richard. She wished she had not had to witness him being brought low like this. He was a good man: weak in some respects – but a good man. And anyway, weren't all men (except, of course, her father) weak?

Antonia had been growing up during the last six months, and she was no longer the callow girl who had arrived in Cape Town at the end of June. But until last night's dramatics, she had sometimes thought that she might truly be in love with Richard. She had certainly felt strongly attracted to him. Now, more than any other emotion, she felt pity for him. Yes – there was still a deep residue of fondness, but pity was the paramount response to his condition. And the thought entered her mind suddenly that she might to some degree have been to blame for it all. But she shook her head and pushed such an idea away.

Richard drove Antonia to D.F. Malan Airport before dawn on the morning of Friday 7th January. The preceding

Tuesday, when the two of them had visited Fish Hoek together to book Antonia's flights, she had visited a few shops while Richard had gone to the bank. (She found him a little while later, as he was sitting reading a newspaper and drinking coffee at Sue's Café). So before she left, she was able to give Miss Chelmsford-Spruce, Mrs. Hapgood, Miss Grogan, and Mrs. Stoddart, a small box of chocolates each. For the staff, she gave Richard fifty Rand in five and ten Rand notes, for him to distribute on her behalf. Antonia was a nicely brought up young woman.

For Richard, on their last evening together, after dinner, she had a tie and a small box of handkerchiefs, along with a greeting card on which she had written: "Dear Richard, Thank you for your hospitality, and for everything you have done for me. I shall never forget you, nor my time here. Please be happy. Love, Antonia."

It was quite a mature note for an eighteen year old girl to have written, although perhaps just a touch condescending. But as we remarked just now, Antonia had done a lot of growing up the last six months. Reading it, Richard felt tears come to his eyes, and he gave Antonia a spontaneous hug, which she returned.

'I really will never forget you, Richard,' she said.

'Nor I you, my darling Antonia,' Richard snuffled.

This very early Friday morning showed promise of turning out to be another lovely high summer's day, but Richard was not feeling at his best. It took him a while to come to his full senses in the morning. He was, invariably, somewhat hung over from the previous evening, and this was certainly the case this morning. Antonia was to take the first connecting flight of the day for Jan Smuts Airport, Johannesburg, then the day-long haul to Heathrow, with the plane refuelling in the Canaries. The previous six days had been a touch awkward for both of them: Richard had been feeling shame, and something horribly like despair. He had drunk prodigious amounts of whiskey during those six days, in an effort to anesthetise his anguish, and it was obvious to many that he was rarely sober. Had it not been for stalwart members of staff such as Elsbet the Cook, Mrs. Stoddart at the front desk in the afternoons (and to a lesser extent, young Jack in the mornings), and André (who performed so many invaluable tasks for Pitlochry House), things would have begun to fall apart at Pitlochry House Hotel that week.

In the departure hall at D.F. Malan Airport, Richard, who always felt a little awkward on occasions like this, took one of Antonia's hands, and kissed her chastely on the cheek. 'I'm glad you visited,' he told her. 'I'm going to miss you.'

'I'm sure we will see each other again someday, Richard,' Antonia responded. Then she too kissed him on the cheek, keeping a hold of his hand. Despite the early hour, there was a large number of people catching the early flight for Johannesburg. She felt very much in the public gaze.

Antonia did not really believe she was likely to see Richard again, not at least for a very long time. She turned once, smiling, as she disappeared through the departure doors, and waved. Richard raised his hand in a salute. Then she was gone, that last image of her lovely face, smiling, to be imprinted on his memory for years to come.

Driving back home, Richard felt numb. He even forgot about the hip flask of whiskey in his pocket. He drove round the back of the house and into the stables yard, where he garaged the car. As he came in via the back door, he saw no one but Bella, going about her mornings chores, and he had to force himself to respond with a polite 'Morning, Bella,' when she greeted him with a smiling '*Môre Meneer*,' and he continued on his way directly to his office, with Katy (who had greeted him in the stables yard) following at his heels. There he closed the door to the room, sat down, and taking the bottle of Bushmills from his desk drawer (he had by now become conscious of a powerful yearning for liquor), he poured a hefty measure into the tumbler, and swallowed it down in two gulps. It was not yet even breakfast time.

Chapter Twenty-One

By 1990, the Apartheid era (the first indications of whose ultimate passing had been foreshadowed by the events of 1976) was very nearly over. The infamous Pass Laws (which had limited freedom of movement for non-whites, and had been the source of so many galling arrests of black people) had been repealed four years earlier, and the last of the Apartheid era laws affecting daily life, the Group Areas Act (which had organised residential neighbourhoods along racial lines, making it illegal to live outside your racially designated neighbourhood), was now widely ignored, its stipulations no longer policed. (It was in fact to be repealed the following year).

In 1990, Richard was fifty-five years old. Although he had long ago foresworn alcohol, he still sometimes had nightmares about the last few years of the 1970s, when his drinking had become totally out of hand, and only the loyalty and dedication of his long serving staff members, in particular, of Elsbet the Cook, her husband, André, and Mrs. Stoddart, had kept the hotel going. And not only the loyalty of his staff, but the loyalty and even affection of some of his long term residential guests.

One mid morning at tea time in 1978, Miss Chelmsford-Spruce had approached Richard on the veranda. He was standing some distance away from the nearest residents, looking out across Noordhoek towards the sea. Katy was lying on the floor next to him.

'Richard,' the old lady addressed him, ' – I may call you Richard?'

Richard, horribly hung over from his excessive drinking the day before, and looking like death, had nodded.

'I have known you for a long time, and I'm more than old enough to be your mother,' the old lady continued. 'And a mother would talk to you now.'

Richard wanted a drink. He had just finished his coffee and had been about to make his way to his office for that purpose, when Miss Chelmsford-Spruce had waylaid him. But the old lady continued, relentless. 'I know that you have had to suffer some personal misfortunes and disappointments the last year or two, but you simply have to play the man and rise above them. You are allowing these misfortunes to break you. And if you are not careful, you will lose everything.'

But Richard had merely given a hollow laugh, and said, 'It seems to me, dear Miss Chelmsford-Spruce, that I have already lost everything.'

'That is simply not true!' the old lady had responded. 'But if you carry on as you are, you will indeed lose everything.'

But Richard had, while feeling both grateful and humbled by Miss Chelmsford-Spruce's intervention, continued to seek oblivion in drink, and he was to suffer increasingly humiliating situations of his own devising, culminating in his finding himself, in early 1979, held in the cells overnight at Fish Hoek Police Station, after having been pulled over late at night for erratic driving, by a police patrol car, as he was on his way back from the Lord Collingwood in Simon's Town. When he got out of the Land Rover, it was immediately clear to the police that he was in no fit state to drive. Fortunately, he had not brought Katy with him. It was only because he was known in the district, and had for many years been respected in the community, that one of the police officers drove Richard's Land Rover to the Police Station for him, rather than simply abandoning it to pillage and theft by the side of the road. Richard had been so drunk that he had felt no shame at the time, not even when he had had to telephone his artist friend from Simon's Town, John, to come collect him in the very early morning. (The Police, although they would not be charging Richard, would not allow him to get into his car as yet). The shame had commenced later that morning, at John's home. (For one look at Richard had decided John that drastic measures were called for, and he had taken his friend back home with him to Simon's Town). By late morning, although Richard was craving a drink desperately, he was technically sober, and consumed by self loathing.

John, Richard's old drinking crony, had some years earlier successfully overcome a drinking problem of his own that had got completely out of hand, since when he had seen comparatively little of Richard, for John now avoided bars. Now, looking at Richard, he saw a wrecked and broken man before him. His friend looked absolutely dreadful, his hair wild, his visage grey, his skin shiny. His hand had trembled as he reached for his coffee cup.

'You know you've reached the end of the road, don't you, Rick?' remarked John. 'I mean, this cannot go on, can it?'

'I know,' Richard responded. 'I don't know what to do.'

'Do you want to stop drinking? Do you admit that you're powerless over alcohol?'

'Yes, I do want to stop drinking. But I seem unable to imagine a life without drink.'

'Then I'm going to help you,' John said. 'Starting now. That is, if you want my help. You can stay here for a few days, while we flush the alcohol out of your system, but you'll have to promise not to go out and get drunk while you're with me. Believe me, the worst will have passed within three days or so.' John smiled at his friend. 'I'm living proof that there can be a happy, productive, alcohol-free life.'

'OK, John. I'll give it a go.'

'That's my boy!'

That afternoon, John had telephoned Mrs. Stoddart at Pitlochry House Hotel, and she had packed a suitcase for Richard – a couple of changes of underwear, a clean and newly pressed pair of trousers, two clean shirts, socks, pyjamas, toiletries, and suchlike – and brought it across that evening. The next three days, Richard found, were truly hellish: he felt burning hot and icy cold all at the same time; he shook and he trembled; he suffered attacks of extreme anxiety and profound self loathing and shame – and he perspired copiously. He could not have kept this up alone, but John nursed him through those three days: he ensured that Richard did not run out of cigarettes; he fed him cups of soup and slices of toast and Bovril; and he provided Richard with as much tea and coffee as he desired. He also made his friend drink vast quantities of sugar-water.

'It's to replace the sugars the alcohol manufactured, and which you are no longer obtaining,' he explained.

Richard smoked two packs of cigarettes a day during those three days. On the fourth day, he began, suddenly, to feel a good deal better. True, he felt weak and frail, utterly drained, but his mind was clear again, and he felt a new determination to make this thing work. So John helped make his friend presentable – Richard had not shaved for three days – and took him to his first Fellowship meeting that evening, and Richard, a salutary reminder to those present of what they had left behind, found himself made welcome, and no one judged him; no one levelled criticisms and condemnation at him.

Who would have guessed that John, who had routinely taken on board even more liquor than Richard in the past, would one day have been the agent of Richard's deliverance? John introduced his friend to a Fellowship that Richard would never have imagined he would one day have need of, let alone find such a sense of community and belonging within. Just as that well known organisation had taught sobriety to John, it now set about saving Richard, and John, who became Richard's sponsor within the Fellowship, led him slowly through the Twelve Steps, and Richard had seized upon sobriety as a drowning man seizes upon a lifebelt. Richard, happily sober now for more than ten years, had become (like his friend, John) that statistically rare creature:

a fully recovered alcoholic, one of the Fellowship's genuine success stories.

It did not bother Richard that alcohol was consumed on the hotel premises; he was not some frothing zealot. What other people chose to do with their lives was none of his affair. (And after all, the sale of alcohol generated a large part of the Pitlochry House Hotel's revenue!) However, Richard shunned alcohol with all the passion of a true convert to sobriety, for his conviction that alcohol was sheer poison for him, was absolute.

In October 1990, Antonia, exhausted, betrayed and broken, fled her ruined marriage. She could not bear to remain in England, with its almost overwhelming associations of personal defeat and great unhappiness, and because her memories of her stay at Pitlochry House thirteen years earlier, and of Richard himself, were now golden ones (the small awkwardness between herself and Richard towards the very end of her stay had been quite forgotten), she once again sought sanctuary in the big house on the mountainside in the Cape Peninsula. As she flew through the night, cocooned in the air-conditioned cabin (why did they turn down the cabin heating at night?), the lights dimmed, the deep roar of the jet engines no longer something that impinged on her consciousness, she told herself that she must expect changes since her previous visit. She hoped however that not too much would have changed. She craved stability and security, in a world where she found both were now absent.

At D.F. Malan Airport, Richard met Antonia's connecting flight from Johannesburg at about eleven in the morning. As she appeared through the arrivals door, he knew her straight away, and his heart skipped a beat, even though this was an older, somewhat worn version of the girl of eighteen he had last seen. She looked pale, exhausted, her features drawn (although that might be due in part to the long overnight flight from London), and she had lost weight. And yet Richard felt the same welling, rising emotion at seeing her again that he had so often felt in 1976: a sensation of sheer joy.

'Antonia!' he called, and she spotted him, suddenly an individual, dear Richard, rather than just another face among a mass of strange faces meeting the flight. She smiled tiredly, and Richard broke ranks and rushed towards her, and without the least conscious thought, he embraced her and kissed her on the cheek. Antonia returned both the embrace and the kiss.

'Antonia! How wonderful to see you again!'

'I can hardly believe I'm here. How are you, Richard?' she asked, smiling again, but this time with a little more animation. She had almost forgotten what a big man Richard was, and he was looking fit, his face glowing with health, his waist trim. How old was he now? Mid-fifties? He did not look it; if anything, he looked in better shape than she remembered – although there was rather more silver at his temples, and perhaps, as his hairline receded, a slightly higher forehead. But these signs of maturity, Antonia thought, suited him.

And Richard answered, 'Very well indeed!' He seized hold of the luggage trolley by one hand, the other behind Antonia's back. 'Let's go home,' he said, 'or do you need to powder your nose? Would you like some coffee first?'

'No, let's go home,' Antonia echoed.

Richard led her to the car, pushing the luggage trolley in front of him. (Gone was the Ford Granada; this was a white Mercedes-Benz E-Class; Helen would have been happy. But Richard and Helen were by now long divorced. Amidst floods of outraged tears, Sonia Van Der Poel had divorced Charles, betrayed both by her closest friend and by her husband, and she had taken up with an athletic young surfer she had picked up on the beach at Kommetjie; Helen, in need of material security – for the divorce court had not awarded her alimony in the no fault divorce she had initiated against Richard – had then married the still wealthy Charles).

Along with sobriety, Richard had acquired a delicacy of character that had not been as pronounced in 1976. It would be Richard – a wiser, more mature, far more thoughtful Richard – who helped rebuild Antonia's self confidence, and who offered her a calmer, far less febrile devotion than he had exhibited in 1976. Together with this devotion came the unconditional love that she so sorely craved and needed. Richard did not ask Antonia probing questions, but over the course of the next week, her story was slowly told: the increasingly unhappy marriage; the bitter divorce once she found out that her husband was routinely cheating on her; her sadness at her childless state. And Richard told her his story: his descent in the late seventies into an alcoholic's Hell; his divorce once the divorce laws were relaxed in 1979 (for Helen had not returned to him a second time); his deliverance from the grip of alcoholism once he had joined the Fellowship (for a while, Richard had baulked at acknowledging the existence of the "Higher Power" that the Fellowship spoke of, let alone confessing his need of help from such a power, but within a few months, his resistance had crumbled, at which time he understood that he truly had been delivered from the compulsion to drink); and his realisation of the value of a long disregarded material asset, to wit, the land he owned and rented out at the foot of the mountain. As Fish Hoek and Noordhoek began in the late seventies to expand in size, and local land values began to climb, this bottom land had become a valuable asset.

Richard had leveraged the sum raised from the sale of the now valuable land to property developers, via a large loan from the bank. (Like all banks, it was ever eager to make a loan when a loan was no longer critically needed). He had been able to renovate and improve Pitlochry House Hotel and its grounds. (For example, every single guest bedroom was now *en suite*, and a lift had been installed). This explained, Richard told Antonia, why the hotel had since acquired two more stars, making it a four-star establishment. (And why there was now a terrace restaurant and a swimming pool!)

'I felt rather bad having to serve my smallholder tenants at the foot of the mountain with eviction notices,' Richard continued, 'but we were slowly going under; I had no real choice. However, I didn't eject the elderly long term residents, and nor did I raise their room rates – '

' – And Miss Chelmsford-Spruce is still here!' interjected Antonia. 'How happy I was to see her again.'

Miss Chelmsford-Spruce, who had always been a supporter of Richard and Antonia, had been equally delighted to see Antonia again. She had an *en suite* room in the new wing (housing the restaurant and its kitchens below, and a number of bedrooms above), built at one end of the hotel in the same architectural style as the original building. Eighty-nine years old now, the last of the old lady residents left, her mind was still astute, and she was far from ready to be despatched to a home for the elderly. In fact, she very much enjoyed the bustle and variety which had marked Pitlochry House Hotel since its renovation and re-launch. But she missed her old crony, Millicent Hapgood, who had died some years ago, and when she went to Holy Communion in Fish Hoek on a Sunday morning, she travelled alone now in the back of the taxi.

In the midsummer warmth of Cape Town in December, Richard and Antonia sat on a shaded bench beneath the Mediterranean pines which grew to one side of the hotel, the warm, still air scented with resin, and Katy II lying at their feet. (Katy I had long gone on to Doggie Heaven, where she occupied herself with chasing tiny Cape Grysbok antelopes, and playing with the other dogs, confident that in due course, her master would join her). Richard, pursuing a rekindled dream that had once been so unlikely of achievement that he had for a long time completely abandoned it, withdrew a small red leather box from his pocket and opened it, revealing a diamond and sapphires ring nestling in white satin, and holding it out to Antonia, he said to her, 'My darling girl, will you marry me?'

'Yes, I will,' responded Antonia, without hesitation, her eyes shining. 'Oh Richard – yes, I *will* marry you!'

Richard felt as if his heart might burst with joy. He

seized Antonia and kissed her passionately – their first true kiss since her return to the Cape.

There are elements of fairy tale in more lives than we would ever imagine.

Richard and Antonia were married in late March the following year. Antonia's mother (her father having died some years ago), along with her brother, flew out for the wedding, both honoured guests at Pitlochry House Hotel. The Bride arrived at Saint Kiaran's Presbyterian Church in Fish Hoek (Divorcées were forbidden to marry in the Anglican Church) in the Cape cart that belonged to Pitlochry House, the conveyance gleaming, varnished and polished. Her brother (whom Richard had carefully coached in driving the Cape cart), sat by her side on the high, leather upholstered seat, the reins in his hands. It was he who gave Antonia away at the start of the service. Richard's friend and saviour, John, acted as his Best Man. After the wedding service, the newly-weds drove off together in the Cape cart for the reception, which was held, of course, at the Pitlochry House Hotel. Richard's son (who had remembered Antonia as an extremely pretty girl much his own age, to whom he had been strongly attracted) had attended the wedding service, and at the reception, he took pleasure in kissing the bride. His presence gratified and pleased his father.

Jeremy, having observed the comparatively sudden success Richard had made of the hotel, an achievement signified by the establishment's acquisition of two extra stars, had at last acquired a degree of respect for his father. When Richard asked him to take charge of the hotel's international marketing and promotion, he agreed with alacrity. He had the good breeding and the innate good taste to appreciate his father's determination to maintain the country house atmosphere of the hotel, and he made much play of Pitlochry House Hotel's unique Old World atmosphere (along with its unique location), in his marketing strategy. What had at first been a mere working *modus vivendi* between father and son had since developed into something a little warmer. But the close bond that had existed between them when Jeremy had been a little boy, would never quite be rekindled. Perhaps that is the case with many fathers and their grown sons.

But as Richard and Antonia set off for their honeymoon in England (what could be more lovely than an English springtime?), where Richard would meet relations new and old, near and distant, he counted his many blessings. And if his relationship with his son fell a little short of the ideal – well, Richard had been taught by the Fellowship to change the things he could, but to accept (in good grace) the things he could not change.

* * * * *

This book is printed on paper from sustainable sources managed under the Forest Stewardship Council (FSC) scheme.

It has been printed in the UK to reduce transportation miles and their impact upon the environment.

For every new title that Troubador publishes, we plant a tree to offset CO_2, partnering with the More Trees scheme.

For more about how Troubador offsets its environmental impact, see www.troubador.co.uk/sustainability-and-community